# THE
# TWILIGHT
# ZONE

# THE TWILIGHT ZONE

BASED ON STORIES BY ROD SERLING,
CHARLES BEAUMONT AND RICHARD MATHESON
ADAPTED BY ANNE WASHBURN

OBERON BOOKS
LONDON

WWW.OBERONBOOKS.COM

First published in 2017 by Oberon Books Ltd
521 Caledonian Road, London N7 9RH
Tel: +44 (0) 20 7607 3637 / Fax: +44 (0) 20 7607 3629
e-mail: info@oberonbooks.com
www.oberonbooks.com

A catalogue record for this book is available from the British Library.

PB ISBN: 9781786824004
E ISBN: 9781786824011

Cover design by Dewynters

Printed and bound by 4EDGE Limited, Hockley, Essex, UK.
eBook conversion by CPI Group (UK) Ltd, Croydon, CR0 4YY.

Visit www.oberonbooks.com to read more about all our books and to
buy them. You will also find features, author interviews and news of
any author events, and you can sign up for e-newsletters so that you're
always first to hear about our new releases.

The following episodes (in alphabetical order) have been adapted for the stage production by Anne Washburn

| Episode | Airdate / Season: | Written By: |
|---|---|---|
| And When the Sky Was Opened | Originally aired December 11, 1959; season 1, episode 11 | Rod Serling based on the short story Disappearing Act by Richard Matheson |
| Eye of the Beholder | Originally aired November 11, 1960; season 2, episode 6 | Rod Serling |
| Little Girl Lost | Originally aired March 16, 1962; season 3, episode 26 | Richard Matheson based on his own short story |
| The Long Morrow | Originally aired January 10, 1964; season 5, episode 15 | Rod Serling |
| Nightmare As A Child | Originally aired April 29, 1960; season 1, episode 29 | Rod Serling |
| Perchance to Dream | Originally aired November 27, 1959; season 1, episode 9 | Charles Beaumont based on his own short story |
| The Shelter | Originally aired September 29, 1961; season 3, episode 3 | Rod Serling |
| Will The Real Martian Please Stand Up? | Originally aired May 26, 1961; season 2, episode 28 | Rod Serling |

## PLAYWRIGHT

**Anne Washburn**'s plays include *10 out of 12*, *Antlia Pneumatica*, *Apparition*, *The Ladies*, *I Have Loved Strangers*, *The Communist Dracula Pageant* and transadaptations of Euripides' *Orestes* and *Iphigenia in Aulis*. Her plays have been produced in the US, and internationally. She is an associated artist with Obie award-winning groups 13P, The Civilians and New Georges, and is an alumna of New Dramatists. *Mr Burns* and *The Internationalist* are also published by Oberon Books.

## ORIGINAL TV SERIES WRITER BIOS.

**Rod Serling** (1924-1975) was born in Syracuse, N.Y. and grew up in Binghamton. While a student at Antioch College in Yellow Springs, Serling sold his first three national radio scripts – and even his first television script. From 1951-1955, more than 70 of his television scripts were produced, garnering both critical and public acclaim. Full-scale success came on Wednesday, January 12th, 1955 with the live airing of his first Kraft Television Theatre script *Patterns*. Deemed a "creative triumph" by critics, and the winner of the first of Serling's six Emmy awards, the acclaimed production was actually remounted live to air a second time on February 9th, 1955 – an unprecedented event. Serling went on to work for CBS' illustrious *Playhouse 90*, for which he crafted 90 minute dramas including the multiple-Emmy Award-winning *Requiem For A Heavyweight*. Serling shocked many of his fans in 1957 when he left *Playhouse 90* to create a science-fiction series he called *The Twilight Zone*. The show debuted in 1959 and CBS would air 156 episodes of the *Twilight Zone*, an astonishing 92 of which were written by Serling over its five year run.

**Charles Beaumont** (1929-1967) was a prolific American author of speculative fiction, including short stories in the horror and science fiction subgenres. He is perhaps best remembered as the writer of many classic *Twilight Zone* episodes (many of them based upon his own short stories), and also penned feature film screenplays, among them *7 Faces of Dr. Lao*, *The Intruder* (based on his own novel) and *The Masque of the Red Death*. As best-selling novelist Dean R. Koontz has said, "[Charles Beaumont was] one of the seminal influences on writers of the fantastic and macabre."

**Richard Matheson** (1926-2013) is the author of many classic novels and short stories. He wrote in a variety of genres including terror, fantasy, horror, paranormal, suspense, science fiction and western. In addition to books, he wrote prolifically for television (including *The Twilight Zone*, *Night Gallery*, *Star Trek*) and numerous feature films. Many of Matheson's novels and stories have been made into movies including *I Am Legend*, *Somewhere in Time*, and *Shrinking Man*. His many awards include the World Fantasy and Bram Stoker Awards for Lifetime Achievement, the Hugo Award, Edgar Award, Spur Award for Best Western Novel, Writer's Guild awards, and in 2010 he was inducted into the Science Fiction Hall of Fame.

The original scripts for *The Twilight Zone* by Rod Serling and Charles Beaumont are available from Gauntless Press and by Richard Matheson from Edge Books (an imprint of Gauntlet Press).

*The Twilight Zone* was first performed at the Almeida Theatre, London, on Tuesday 5 December 2017 with the following cast and creative team:

*Cast*

| | |
|---|---|
| **Driver/Rathmann/Phil/Forbes/Martin** | Oliver Alvin-Wilson |
| **High Strung/Ruth/Sandy/Mrs Martin/Nurse** | Franc Ashman |
| **Little Girl/Markie/Lily** | Adrianna Bertola |
| **Maja/Ethel/Mrs Weiss/Bandaged Lady** | Lizzy Connolly |
| **Respectable/Helen/Grace/General Walters** | Amy Griffiths |
| **Stockton/Seldon/Bixler/Big Headed Alien** | Neil Haigh |
| **Crank/Greg/Gart/Henderson** | Cosmo Jarvis |
| **Hall/The Narrator/Ross** | John Marquez |
| **Perry/Harlowe/Harrington/Police Doctor/Adjunct** | Matthew Needham |
| **Haley/The Bartender/Stansfield/Weiss/Lieutenant** | Sam Swainsbury |
| **Supernumeraries** | Keith Biley |
| | Ed Fredenburgh |
| | Ian Recordon |

*Please note that the text of the play which appears in this volume may be changed during the rehearsal process and appear in a slightly altered form in the performance.*

*Creative team*

| | |
|---|---|
| **Adaptation** | Anne Washburn |
| **Direction** | Richard Jones |
| **Design** | Paul Steinberg |
| **Costume** | Nicky Gillibrand |
| **Choreography** | Aletta Collins |
| **Light** | Mimi Jordan Sherin |
| **Composition and Sound** | Sarah Angliss |
| **Sound** | Christopher Shutt |
| **Music Direction** | Stephen Bentley-Klein |
| **Musicians** | Sarah Angliss, Stephen Bentley-Klein, Stephen Hiscock |
| **Costume Supervision** | Deborah Andrews |
| **Casting** | Julia Horan CDG |
| **Dialect** | Danièle Lydon |
| **Fight Direction** | Bret Yount |
| **Associate Director** | Joe Austin |
| **Associate Sound Designer** | Zoe Milton |
| **Associate Designer** | Dilâra Medin |
| **Resident Director** | Tom Brennan |
| **Illusions** | Richard Wiseman and Will Houstoun |
| **Company Stage Manager** | Kate McDowell |
| **Deputy Stage Manager** | Rebecca Maltby |
| **Assistant Stage Manager** | Abi Cook/ Kieran Watson |

Based on stories by Rod Serling, Charles Beaumont and Richard Matheson.

**Ron Fogelman**

Producer for Your Next Stop Limited.

Ron is a producer, writer and specialist adviser to the entertainment industry working across Theatre, Film and TV.

Sound is crucial, and should be extraordinary as often as possible.

*Footsteps in snow, very loud*

*The sound of wind brushing lightly over a field of snow – magnified*

*The faint sound of the aurora borealis: radio waves and chiming*

*The sound of the prickle of snow in the wind*

*We hear the sound of a man's breath, in winter*

*We are hearing a man paused in a snowfield enrapt by the stars and troubled by the dark*

*Footsteps crunching on snow*

*A state trooper enters a diner.*

HALEY: Coffee?

PERRY: That bus out there – whose is it?

DRIVER: That's mine, officer, what's the problem?

PERRY: The bridge ahead, they've declared it: 'temporarily impassible'. Ice flow stacked up. Another pound of weight and it could be driftwood.

DRIVER: That's rough.

PERRY: Looks like you're kind of marooned. 'Til morning anyway.

ROSS: 'Til morning! But I've got to be in Boston at 9 a.m.! I've got a very important meeting!

DRIVER: You can start walking, Mister, but you're gonna need snowshoes.

PERRY: That slide back there at the turnoff has blocked the whole road. You might as well all get comfortable and get a little hot food in you.

ROSS: Oh that's just great. That's fine, isn't it? Get comfortable, and get a little hot food in me. That's precious consolation for missing my meeting. *(He laughs sardonically.)* That's a fine little bus line you work for, isn't it? They care so much about their schedules, don't they?

DRIVER: I wouldn't be too hard on them Mister. They have no control over the snow, bridges, the sides of hills that decide to come down. That's all pretty much out of their hands.

*ROSS harrumphs.*

*There is a long pause while PERRY eyes the passengers, one by one; for the most part they return his gaze, with mild apprehension or puzzlement.*

*After a moment:*

HALEY: Something wrong, Perry?

PERRY: There a back door to this place?

HALEY: Sure is.

*A beat.*

PERRY: Maybe you wouldn't mind going back there and locking it.

HALEY: It's already locked.

PERRY: Thanks. Tell me, who was it was in here before the bus stopped?

HALEY: Why … nobody. I haven't served anybody since 11 o'clock this morning.

*A beat.*

PERRY: Driver, you got a passenger manifest?

DRIVER: Passenger manifest? What do you think I got parked out there a 707? Mister, that's a fourteen-year-old bus and business is lousy. My boss would run rum across the border if there was profit in it. We don't ask passengers their names. We kiss them gently and help them in we're that glad to have them.

PERRY: Do you know how many you had?

DRIVER: Six. Unless one fell out a window when we hit a bump. Six's what I picked up, and six's what I'm supposed to deliver.

PERRY: Nobody fell out. Somebody jumped in. There are seven here now.

*There is a small prickle of sound from the jukebox.*

DRIVER: That's funny. I know I had six people. I counted heads before we took off. There were six.

PERRY: Then how do you account for the seven?

DRIVER: That one beats me. One of them didn't get off the bus.

*A beat.*

PERRY: Which one of you wasn't on the bus?

*There is a pause.*

RESPECTABLE: Oh this is ridiculous. Surely we were *all* on the bus.

ROSS: Is this an interrogation? Because if we're going to be grilled, I hope you intend to supply a lawyer.

*He folds his arms, leans back in his chair with his legs stuck deliberately out.*

CRANK: That's a good one. First he wants snowshoes, then he wants a lawyer. *(Cackles.)*

ROSS: I don't remember seeing *you* on the bus.

CRANK: Well that's a holler. Because I don't remember seeing you neither. *(Cackles.)*

HIGH STRUNG LADY: This is ridiculous. What difference does it make who was on the bus or who wasn't, or whether there were six or seven or a hundred and twenty?

PERRY: Now take it easy Lady.

HALEY: What's this all about?

PERRY: You didn't hear anything flying over here tonight?

HALEY: Flying over here? I didn't hear anything.

3

PERRY: We got a call about two hours ago. Woman said she heard something fly over and then come down.

HALEY: Nothing's come down here except snow. That's all I've seen for the past fourteen hours. Snow.

PERRY: Well … something did land in Tracy's Pond. Left a trail of broken branches before it hit.

ROSS: Something like *what* pray tell.

PERRY: We don't know yet. They'll dredge it out in the morning when Hank's tow finishes up with the slide.

CRANK: An *unidentified* flying object – I make that a U.F.O! *(Cackles.)*

PERRY: We found tracks in the snow, leading away.

HALEY: Tracks, huh.

HIGH STRUNG: Where did they lead to??

PERRY: Here. They led here.

*A frozen moment. A voice from nowhere.*

*At the same time, a cigarette on the counter kindles and smokes.*

THE NARRATOR: Wintry February night, the present. Order of events: a phone call from a frightened woman, a state trooper, a sunken object in an icy pond – but nothing more enlightening to add beyond tracks leading across the highway to a diner. You've heard of trying to find a needle in a haystack? Well stay with us now, and you'll be part of an investigation whose mission is to find – not that proverbial needle, no, the task is even harder. Officer Dan Perry has got to find an alien in a diner, and you'll search with him, because you've just landed in –

HALEY: *(Laughing.)* That's crazy. Nothing's come in here since 11:00 this morning.

DRIVER: Except me and my passengers. Me and six people. That means that one person here –

RESPECTABLE: Now, let me get this straight. You're trying to tell us that someone landed in a kind of flying saucer, or something, and then came in here?

HIGH STRUNG: Came in here with us?

LITTLE GIRL: *Who* landed in a flying saucer?

RESPECTABLE: Hush.

ROSS: Well that's just not possible. We'd have seen them.

RESPECTABLE: I don't know that we would have. In the snow and the dark. We climbed off that bus in a hurry to get out of the storm.

HIGH STRUNG: Anyone could have slipped in with us, we wouldn't have noticed.

PERRY: You were all on the bus together.

*They all look around at each other.*

DRIVER: *(Somewhat reluctantly.)* They loaded in a snow storm in Hooks Landing. To tell the truth, I don't know who got on, I was just hustling to get them in in the first place. And the heater on that bus, it isn't the finest –

RESPECTABLE: I'll say.

DRIVER: Everyone was just sort of huddled up in their coats. Couldn't really see anybody in the dim.

CRANK: Just like a science fiction is what it is. A regular Ray Bradbury. Six humans and one monster from outer space. *(Turns to ROSS.)* You wouldn't happen to have an eye in the back of your head would you? *(Cackles madly.)*

ROSS: I find you offensive, do you know that?

CRANK: Most Martians do, Mister, most Martians do! *(Cackles.)*

*There's a beat.*

RESPECTABLE: Well officer … what now?

ROSS: Yes just what is standard police procedure for an alien invasion in a two-bit greasy spoon in the middle of nowhere.

HALEY: Why hey there.

ROSS: I'm so interested to know.

PERRY: Well …

*He looks around.*

This isn't exactly par for our courses I'll admit it. We go off on a lot of nutty assignments but this one – wow.

HIGH STRUNG: Well we've got to find out who it is don't we? Don't we?

*A brief moment where everyone eyes everyone else.*

LITTLE GIRL: You should be using deductive reasoning. I mean, it's only logical.

CRANK: That's right girlie – you go get 'em!

PERRY: You got identification Mister?

CRANK: Left it under the pod on my spaceship.

*A beat.*

PERRY: Who won the world series last year?

ROSS: This is an Abbot and Costello routine in the making.

CRANK: I got it! I got it! Sharp boy, but I got it! Pittsburg Pirates won it. Took four out of seven from the Yankees – didn't figure us Martians would know anything about the Great American Pastime, did you, huh?

*He cackles madly.*

PERRY: What about you, miss. You got identification?

ETHEL: Well … no. As a matter of fact, I don't. I left my wallet – I left it in my suitcase. It was shipped on ahead.

PERRY: What's your name, Miss?

ETHEL: Ethel McConnell. I'm a professional dancer.

CRANK: How many legs? How many legs?

ETHEL: I'm going to belt you, grandpa.

DRIVER: She was on the bus.

PERRY: How do you know?

DRIVER: She's the only one I noticed.

ETHEL: Well … thank you.

CRANK: Sure but who noticed him?

*He cackles madly.*

How do we know you're the same one that was driving the bus, huh? Ain't nobody been exonerated yet, that's for sure. Least of all that suspicious little girl. Hey there suspicious little girl, what's in your suspicious suitcase, eh?

*The LITTLE GIRL touches the big wooden case by her feet protectively.*

HIGH STRUNG: Oh hey leave the sweet kid alone. Her mama can vouch for her.

LITTLE GIRL: Oh no, Ma'am. I'm traveling alone.

CRANK: And what if one of us *is* an alien from outer space. Far as I know there's nothing in the constitution says you can't be an alien from outer space. Not if you aren't bothering nobody.

ROSS: Look, let's cut this farce out right now. We'll all show our identification and put a stop to it. The whole thing's ridiculous.

*The lights flicker for a few moments.*

HIGH STRUNG: What was that?

*Micropause.*

DRIVER: Probably just snow. On the power cables.

*Jukebox switches over to another kind of music entirely, one you would not expect to find in a jukebox.*

*The volume increases and increases then:*

*the juke switches back to the peppy era-specific dance music which tootles along in a bland and cheery fashion.*

*A meaty pause.*

PERRY: Haley … this isn't your idea of a gag is it?

HALEY: Not me.

*CRANK nears the jukebox and then salutes it, laughing manically.*

CRANK: Take me to your leader! Take me to your leader!

*Lights go out entirely. Jukebox cuts out. HIGH STRUNG LADY screams briefly.*

*Bit of a pause.*

DRIVER: Power's out.

PERRY: *(Grimly.)* Maybe.

CRANK: Maybe not …

PERRY: Everyone stay right where you are.

*A moment, they all wait, bated breath.*

*Another meaty pause.*

PERRY: We may get a laugh out of all of this in the morning.

ETHEL: I wish whoever it was would play his cards right now – why don't they *do* something?

RESPECTABLE: I would just as soon, that they did *not*.

HIGH STRUNG: Maybe they're just … playing around.

THE MAN WHO HASN'T SPOKEN UNTIL NOW: Cat and mouse.

*A sort of a pause.*

RESPECTABLE: What if the thing *doesn't* show itself? Do we just sit here, holding our breath?

PERRY: I think it's safe to say that nobody understands what's going on.

ROSS: Childish nonsense.

HALEY: You got a better explanation?

ROSS: I do indeed. Snow on the power lines. Shoddy electronics. And our driver – not a paragon of acuity –

DRIVER: Hey.

ROSS: – is mistaken. Seven people got on the bus and he, distracted by our glamorous friend here, thought there were only six.

*Lights suddenly bump up extra bright and the jukebox plays a boisterous and thoroughly 21st century tune.*

*Some shrieking.*

*Suddenly the sound of a great and momentous pounding.*

*This sound originates in the jukebox but then and perhaps quite suddenly comes from all about them, people may be a bit cowering behind chairs half crouched under tables.*

*The phone rings.*

*The lights slide back to a cheery normal, and the jukebox swaps instantly to a pleasant jaunty period-specific tune*

*there is a long … period … of time …*

*the inhabitants of the diner uncurl from whatever stance of self protection they had assumed*

9

*they are glancing amongst themselves, looking to PERRY*

*the phone continues to ring*

*and ring*

*finally they hear it properly.*

DRIVER: *(Hoarse.)* Someone going to answer that?

*He is looking at HALEY as he does so.*

*HALEY looks at PERRY.*

*PERRY gears himself up and picks up the phone.*

PERRY: Hello?

*Pause while everyone strains to hear.*

Uh huh. That's right? *(Pause.)* Well … alright then.

*He hangs up the phone. Clears his throat. Turns around.*

*A brief pause.*

That was the county engineer. They've checked out that bridge … it's been declared passable.

*A pause.*

DRIVER: Well …

ROSS: *(Assembles himself.)* It's about time.

DRIVER: I guess we … go now?

PERRY: Well … I guess so.

ROSS: Hallelujah.

RESPECTABLE: And that's just going to be the … end of that?

CRANK: *(Serious, for once.)* You're making a mistake, officer. A big mistake. You're letting a monster out.

*A beat. Everyone strains forward.*

PERRY: That may be. That may well be. But you can't hold anyone on suspicion of being a monster.

*(To the DRIVER.)* You can roll them at any time.

DRIVER: *(Clears his throat.)* They're sure about that bridge.

ROSS: That bridge just got a clean bill of health and you'll drive that bus right across.

DRIVER: Listen Mister. You may be a big shot in Boston, but when it comes to bridges and buses, I got seniority, and I tell you that bridge is so old that –

PERRY: I'm going to go on ahead in the car. Cross the bridge first.

HALEY: Alright. You can pay for your checks right here, ladies and gentlemen.

*There is a sort of pause. HALEY takes charge.*

Now you had the chili and saltines, right? That's ninety cents.

*RESPECTABLE comes forward resolutely, reaches into her purse and produces the amount.*

Thank you. And you had – what – fourteen cups of coffee? That's a dollar forty. You had the pie – that will be fifty-five cents please. Two cups of coffee and a doughnut that's thirty cents … an ice cream sundae with extra ice cream extra sprinkles and with extra fudge sauce that will be forty cents for you, young lady. Thank you very much.

*As he reels off their orders they crowd around and fall into the soothing routine of bill payment.*

*Over that:*

ETHEL: Goodbye, officer.

PERRY: Miss McConnell.

ETHEL: It strikes me that you aren't entirely sorry to see the back end of our little dilemma.

*He tips his hat.*

PERRY: Boston your final destination?

ETHEL: I have employment in New York City.

PERRY: New York City. I always thought I might visit. Take in the sights. See a show.

I have some time off in a few weeks. I don't suppose you'll be performing then, Miss McConnell?

ETHEL: Oh I really wish that were the case Officer Perry. But I'm afraid it's a strictly private affair.

*She has pulled a cigarette from her pocket book and placed it absently between her lips*

PERRY: Oh here, allow *(He's rummaging.)* me.

*He clicks his lighter on, holds it out, she stares at it uncomprehendingly.*

Unless you'd rather leave it unlit.

*She looks at him. He gestures towards her face. She puts her fingers up and finds the cigarette, looks at it.*

ETHEL: Oh. Oh how very strange.

PERRY: Not your usual brand?

ETHEL: I don't smoke.

PERRY: That was how it was when I quit. Tense moment, and I'd find I'd rooted one out from somewhere.

ETHEL: No, I mean. I haven't ever smoked.

*As she follows the line of passengers exiting.*

I don't even know how.

HALEY: Godspeed, and a safe trip. And you all come back and see us again, you hear? That is, all but one of you … …

DRIVER: Well. That's seven of them.

PERRY: *(Absently.)* Yup.

CRANK: *(On his way out the door.)* Bet you by the time we get to
  Boston there's seventeen.

*He cackles but it's a different cackle. Mordant.*

*The LITTLE GIRL is the last one out. She pauses, waves, turns to go.*

*The bell on the door jingles as she exits.*

*The bell mingles with the clanging of a knife on a water glass –
HALEY has reached up and turned on the television above the counter.*

*As the lights start to dim we hear:*

*A pleasing demi-party hubbub.*

*The clanging of a spoon against a glass.*

*We see on the television set a black and white image of a dinner
party in a suburban home:*

HARLOWE: Ladies and gentlemen … ladies and gentlemen
  may I have your attention please!

No birthday celebration is complete without an after-
dinner speech!

*Laughter and applause.*

And so to get to the business at hand which is the honoring
of one Dr. William Stockton who's grown one year older
and will admit to being over twenty-one!

*More laughter.*

And who in the short space of twenty years has taken care
of us, our kids, even our grandkids!

DR. STOCKTON: *(With a grin.)* You dirty dog you! First
  a surprise party – which I abhor. And that sloppy
  sentimental speech!

*Again laughter, humorous protests etc.*

*On the counter, the discarded cigarette glows briefly to life, emits a long plume of smoke.*

*HAYLEY reaches upward with a remote control and switches the TV off.*

*We are plunged into the dark:*

TINA: Maaaaama!

*The sound of two sleeping adults slowly half rousing.*

GREG: I'll get it.

RUTH: *(Bleary.)* You going?

GREG: *(Still all but asleep.)* Just putting on my slippers.

TINA: Maaamaaa!

GREG: Alright sweetheart.

*We hear, magnified, the sound of slipper tread on carpet.*

*Dog starts to bark outside.*

*(Sleepy.)*

What's up Mack?

*We hear a door open.*

Tina?

What's the matter honey … .

*A moment.*

*Muffled: the sound of the dog barking outside, frantic.*

*The sound of a lightswitch.*

*After a moment:*

… Tina?

TINA: *(More of a whimper.)* Maaamaaa.

*After a moment:*

GREG: Ruth! Ruthie!

*During the intro the lights have slowly come up on a NURSE leading a WOMAN whose face is entirely bandaged.*

*The NURSE – whose face we cannot see – begins to unbandage the WOMAN whose own hands hover in a mixture of anticipation and apprehension.*

*A LITTLE GIRL sits on the edge of the stage.*

*HELEN, an attractive composed woman in her late twenties is in the act of pulling out the keys to her apartment when she sees her.*

HELEN: Well, hello there. Do you live on this floor? Or are you just visiting someone?

*The LITTLE GIRL looks up at her. But does not speak.*

You're rather quiet.

Not much to say?

Or maybe … you have a lot to say. And you just choose to not say it.

I'm kind of an expert on children you see. Quiet ones and noisy ones – all kinds. I teach school.

MARKIE: I know.

HELEN: *(Amused.)* Oh you do, do you. Did one of the kids in the building tell you that. Well, would you like some hot chocolate while you wait?

On cold afternoons when I come back from school … that's the first thing I like to do. Make myself a nice cup of hot chocolate. Would you like one?

MARKIE: *(Firmly.)* No marshmallows.

HELEN: Oh you don't like marshmallows do you.

MARKIE: No I don't.

HELEN: You know what? I don't like them either. Even when I was your age I didn't like them. So that's a pair of us.

Come on inside and I'll put the milk on – but shouldn't you tell your mother I've invited you? I wouldn't want her to be worried.

MARKIE: She won't be.

*Darkness and the sound of a dog barking.*

*Lights up on a little girl's bed.*

*GREG stands in the middle of the room.*

*RUTH has appeared in the doorway in a wrapper, yawning.*

RUTH: Greg, what is it?

*After a moment.*

GREG: I don't know.

*He turns to look at her, after a moment she takes in his look. Panic begins to rise ever so slightly.*

RUTH: Where's Tina?

*Another moment.*

GREG: She's not here.

RUTH: *(Mild exasperation: dumb men.)* Well but she, she must be sleepwalking she's in the living room or –

*She moves towards the door.*

*From mid air:*

TINA: *(Sleepy.)* Mama?

*A moment.*

*RUTH strides to the bed and sweeps the covers aside (although they very clearly conceal nothing).*

*A moment.*

*She drops to the floor to look under the bed then springs up again. She is frantic, but hushed as though instinctively concealing her panic from her daughter.*

RUTH: Where *is* she?

GREG: I don't know.

*(On the verge of panicking.)* Honey, we're not going to panic.

*The dog, outside, is barking like mad.*

Shut up, Mack!

Darling I'm going to call Phil.

RUTH: *Phil?*

GREG: He's a physicist; he may be able to help.

*He exits the room.*

*RUTH buries her face in her hands.*

*Darkness and the dog barking.*

*There is something kind of weird about the barking dog.*

*In the darkness we hear:*

FORBES: *(In agony.)* Tom, there were three of us in that ship, three of us. You and me and a Colonel named Harrington.

GART: Harrington.

FORBES: Ed Harrington. He was thirty-six years old. He was my best friend. I'd known him for fifteen years and you'd known him for five.

GART: Forbes … I don't *know* any Ed Harrington.

*LIGHTS UP abruptly on MARKIE in a big chair, holding a cup of hot chocolate and HELEN settling herself in a chair opposite.*

HELEN: It isn't too rich, is it?

17

MARKIE: It's okay.

   I'm glad it isn't too hot.

   I don't like hot things.

   Do you?

HELEN: Like hot things? No. No I don't actually.

MARKIE: When I was a little girl I was playing near the stove, and a pot of hot tea fell off of it.

   Why don't you like hot things?

HELEN: *(Faintly amused by the turn the conversation is taking.)* Oh … well. I don't actually know why I don't like hot things

MARKIE: You don't remember?

HELEN: There are a lot of things I'm … vague about. From when I was a certain age. Things I don't really recall.

MARKIE: Don't you?

HELEN: You know it's not very polite to … to –

MARKIE: *(Interrupting.)* Sometimes do people look like you know them already?

HELEN: Do they –

MARKIE: *(Finds the word.)* Familiar. Do sometimes people look familiar to you?

HELEN: Well I mean of course, yes. Sometimes.

MARKIE: Today?

HELEN: Today? Why, no.

MARKIE: Really?

HELEN: You know, it's not very polite to just contradict people. I just told you I didn't –

   *Stops, held a moment.*

Yes. Yes actually there was. But –

*She moves to mentally dismiss it from her thoughts.*

Outside the school. Crossing the street. There was a man in a car. Stopped for a light. I saw his face through the windshield.

MARKIE: Who is the man?

HELEN: Who is he? Oh … I don't know. No he wasn't someone I recognized he just looked so … so …

MARKIE: Familiar.

HELEN: He did. But I couldn't say why. *(Deciding to be educational:)* But that's just something which happens sometimes.

MARKIE: I don't like him.

HELEN: You don't like him – who is he?

MARKIE: I can't. I can't remember! But I know … I know he's frightening.

*Bit of a hung pause.*

HELEN: Who are you? Where do you live?

MARKIE: Markie. But that's not my real name. But that's what people call me.

They call me Markie!

HELEN: Yes, yes I heard you.

MARKIE: Markie!

HELEN: It's a pretty name. A very pretty name.

MARKIE: Yes, and?

Yes and?

HELEN: It's a cute name –

*Offstage: sound of an elevator door opening.*

*Sound of footsteps.*

MARKIE: *(Whispering.)* Oh … he's coming …

HELEN: *Who* is coming?

MARKIE: I don't I don't I don't I can't *remember* …

*Footsteps approach, stop.*

I have to go I have to go go out the back way –

HELEN: Honey there's nothing to be afraid of.

MARKIE: Yes. There *is.*

*She runs offstage and we hear a door slam.*

*The doorbell rings.*

*HELEN stares at it.*

*Sound of New York City at noon in the Fifties, cars etc.*

*Just as that establishes the jukebox begins to glow.*

*And from it emanates the sound of the carnival, slowly increasing until the noon day city furor bleeds into:*

*Merry-go-round music*

*Screams*

*Squeals*

*Pop-pop of rifles*

*Clack-clack of an ascending roller coaster*

MAJA: *(In a loud but intimate whisper to the audience.)* Now is the time to do all of the things you can't do when you're awake!

*Among the carnival din we hear, loud but far away and echo-y*

RATHMANN: Mr. Hall.

*Carnival continues but dwindles*

Mr. Hall.

*until it cuts out abruptly with:*

Mr. Hall!

*Lights bump abruptly on full to HALL and DR. RATHMANN.*

*Again the faint sounds of the city.*

RATHMANN: You were drifting off there for a moment Mr. Hall – you aren't feeling ill are you?

HALL: No. Just tired.

I'm the tiredest man in the world.

You know how long I've been awake?

Eighty-seven hours. Almost four days, and four nights.

RATHMANN: And you can't go to sleep, is that it?

*HALL laughs. A little long, and a little maniacal.*

HALL: *Can't?* No, doctor, that isn't it. *Mustn't.*

I must not go to sleep.

Because if I do go to sleep … I'll never wake up.

*Rises from chair.*

You don't mind if I walk around, do you?

RATHMANN: Stand on your head if you think it'll help.

*HALL chuckles.*

What's funny now?

HALL: You are. You're sure you're a psychiatrist?

RATHMANN: Why do you ask?

HALL: I don't know. I guess I expected something different.

RATHMANN: Like an old man with a white beard and a Cherman agg-zent?

HALL: Maybe.

*RATHMANN puts on a pair of glasses.*

RATHMANN: Feel more comfortable?

HALL: You're okay. But I'm afraid I'm wasting your time. You can't help me.

RATHMANN: You're sure of that.

HALL: Yeah.

RATHMANN: If I can't help you, then why come to me?

HALL: Fred Jackson, my regular doctor. He insisted.

RATHMANN: Yes he called me with the referral.

HALL: And I thought – why not give it a try. I mean: why not. But now that I'm here … well it's obvious you can't help me. Nothing personal. No one can help me.

RATHMANN: Mr. Hall. Do you think running away will do you any good? Don't get me wrong. Sometimes running away is the best answer. But I don't know that yours is that sort of problem. Maybe it is, and maybe it isn't. You can do what you like, but I'm going to sock you for twenty-five bucks no matter what.

*There's a sort of a pause.*

HALL: You promise you won't put me in a straight jacket.

RATHMANN: I don't promise anything.

HALL: Not that that would make a difference anyway.

RATHMANN: Then get on with it. Start anywhere.

HALL: Okay. Alright.

But I'm warning you: you're going to think I've lost my marbles.

RATHMANN: Marbles can be found, Mr. Hall. Go on.

HALL: You asked for it.

Let me think about the best way to tell this – you won't believe me in any case but, I may as well make it a good story.

*His eyes droop for a moment; we hear the carnival music.*

RATHMANN: Mr. Hall? You were drifting off again.

*His eyes snap open, the carnival music ceases.*

HALL: I had a long illness when I was fifteen. I developed a rheumatic heart. You know what that means Doc, it's a life sentence. They said I'd never really be entirely well, that I'd have to take it easy from then on. No strenuous exercise, long walks, stairs. No shocks. Shock produces too much adrenaline, they said. Bad. Avoid any kind of surprise. And I've done … all of that. Followed all the advice. I lead a very dull life.

Not the life I used to … imagine, I would lead.

I wonder if you've ever really thought about the imagination, Doctor.

RATHMANN: It does fall into my job description.

HALL: Sure. Nuts and kooks. People who believe things which just aren't so. But when you were a little kid, doctor, *you* believed things that weren't so – Santa Claus, I mean, and, things under the bed, monsters in the closet no one could talk you out of; maybe you had a teddy bear and maybe you thought it had … feelings, it was important to consider. You get the picture.

RATHMANN: Sure. I'll admit to all of that. Only it wasn't a teddy bear it was a toy robot.

*HALL laughs briefly.*

HALL: I like you, doctor. I bet if anyone could help me, it would be you. Only you can't help me. I hope you don't take it personally.

23

RATHMANN: As far as I'm concerned, the jury's still out on that. You were talking about the imagination.

HALL: The imagination. That thing we don't mind little kids having, actually we think it's adorable, children and their crazy beliefs. Gets a big laugh, a sentimental tear. But we don't like an adult to have too much imagination. And me, I've got a lot of it.

RATHMANN: A large imagination can be an asset for an adult, too. As long as you're able to distinguish what is real, from what isn't real – is that a problem for you?

HALL: Oh I can tell what's real and what isn't real. I know the difference. But what about the Imaginary. You tell me this, Doc – does the *Imaginary* know the difference?

*Tiny beat.*

RATHMANN: Dextroamphetamine?

HALL: How else do you think I've been able to stay awake?

RATHMANN: How many grains a day?

HALL: That would be telling. Oh I don't know. Thirty, thirty-five.

RATHMANN: I'm going to have to let Doctor Jackson know.

HALL: Go ahead. I don't have much longer anyway.

RATHMANN: Alright. Now that we're square. Maybe you'd better tell me how this all began.

*HALL exhales, stares into space a moment. Just as RATHMANN is about to lean forward and say something, HALL begins.*

HALL: It started a week ago. I went to bed around ten. I wasn't too tired, but, my heart, I need the rest. I always go to bed around ten.

*Merry-go-round music*

*clack-clack of roller coaster*

*screams …*

*Lights are fading.*

*The jukebox glows.*

*Carnival is increasing*

*We hear HALL's voice on the overhead speaker:*

I don't even know when I went to sleep. But all of a sudden I wasn't home any more

I was at a carnival. It was crowded, people were all around me, pushing, yelling …

*Sound of a crowd, a fairground:*

BARKER: Hey, buddy, c'mere. C'mon! Hey! Six shots for a dime hit the bull's eye you get a kewpie doll come on how about it ten cents ten pennies.

*Abruptly there is a pounding – this is the same pounding we heard earlier in the diner – and we are plunged into total darkness, the carnival whisked away.*

*A pounding that horrible pounding.*

*And then abruptly, that horrible pounding stops.*

*The jukebox – which has been glowing radiantly, infernally, with the carnival and the pounding –*

*extinguishes.*

*We hear the chime of a completely civilized doorbell.*

*At the same time the lights come up on HELEN, standing in the middle of her room, the two empty chairs nearby, staring panicked at the door offstage.*

*The doorbell rings again.*

HELEN: *(Voice almost shaking.)* Who is it?

SELDEN: *(From behind the door.)* Miss Foley? Miss Helen Foley?

It's Peter Selden, Miss Foley.

I don't know whether you remember me or not … I knew
your mother very well.

HELEN: My mother …

*She pauses just for a microsecond then she goes and opens the door.*

SELDEN: *(Offstage.)* Do you remember me?

HELEN: *(Offstage.)* You … you do look familiar. Didn't I see
you – ?

SELDEN: *(Laughs.)* I thought you looked at me a little oddly.
Yes, that's right, in front of the school. I was stopped for a
red light. Do you mind if I come in for a moment?

HELEN: Why no … no … please do.

*They enter the room.*

SELDEN: It's been a lot of years, Miss Foley. Eighteen or
nineteen to be exact. *(Laughs.)* Got you stumped, huh?
Well it's no wonder. You were just a little girl then. You
couldn't have been more than ten or eleven. I used to work
for your mother. Selden. Any bells? Peter Selden?

You were ill I know, for a long time, after the tragedy. I
heard you lost a lot of your memory. I suppose I must have
been swallowed up along with everything else.

HELEN: I'm so sorry I'm afraid I have only vague disjoined
*impressions* really from that … part of my life.

SELDEN: Terrible time. A very terrible time. You moved
to Chicago afterwards didn't you? I seem to remember
someone telling me that.

HELEN: Yes, I lived with an aunt there. I've only been back for
a few weeks or so. I started teaching at the school here in
September.

*Somewhat disconnectedly staring at him.*

I teach school now.

26

SELDEN: I heard that. I was coming through town on business and someone who used to know your mother pointed you out to me and … well I felt I had to stop and just say hello. Especially because, well it did seem as though you might have recognized me, stopped at that light. I always used to wonder what had become of you.

HELEN: And you worked for my mother. It's so strange that I can't seem to recall your name at all.

SELDEN: I worked for her for almost a year, until … I handled her investments.

HELEN: Selden, you say?

SELDEN: That's right. Selden. But it's wonderful to know that you've grown up the way you have. I was quite a favorite of yours but … I suppose you don't remember that either.

HELEN: No. No, I'm sorry.

SELDEN: I lived in the same apartment building and you would pop by. I would make you hot chocolate and we would have grand chats. You're quite certain you don't remember any of this?

*She shakes her head.*

No I was positively a favorite with you. That's why I felt I must look you up when I found you were in town.

HELEN: *(As if this might ring a bell.)* You lived in the same building.

SELDEN: I did. Just down the hall. I heard you screaming that night and I was the first one to … well. The first one to arrive on the scene. Miserable, tragic, terrible thing.

HELEN: Yes. I mean of course it was. This will seem strange to you but it just sort of left my mind, all of it. All I remember is a kind of vague nightmarish thing, waking up in bed, hearing my mother scream, seeing this … this person –

SELDEN: You saw his face?

HELEN: I don't … know. I don't know if I actually saw his face. If I did it's one of the things I've forgotten or at least pushed out of my mind. Are you here for a while, Mr. Selden?

SELDEN: No. I'm just passing through.

HELEN: So you said – I forgot. Please, I'm delighted you stopped. You wouldn't care for coffee or … or cocoa, or –

*She looks down at the cup left behind and stops, fixed.*

SELDEN: Something the matter, Miss Foley?

HELEN: That's odd. She'd almost finished her cocoa … or at least I thought she had. But it's absolutely untouched. That *is* odd. But then she's a rather odd little thing.

SELDEN: Who is?

HELEN: Oh this very funny little creature I found camped out by my door when I came in this afternoon. Strange little girl, Markie. She lives somewhere in the building.

SELDEN: Markie? *Really?* Markie?

HELEN: Oh that isn't her real name, it's just her nickname.

SELDEN: But Miss Foley, that was *your* nickname, when you were a little girl. Markie.

HELEN: … Markie …

SELDEN: What a funny coincidence.

HELEN: Markie … that's right I *was* called Markie. I haven't thought of that in years, but that *is* what people called me wasn't it?

SELDEN: I'm sure that given time you'll remember a lot of things. Didn't the doctors tell you that your memories would come back, eventually?

HELEN: They didn't know.

Markie. What a strange thing to have forgotten.

SELDEN: Now that you're back here, in the town you grew up in, surrounded by familiar sights, and people who used to know you, I'm sure it will all gradually come back to you. Bit by bit. Like puzzle pieces, slowly adding up to a picture.

HELEN: I almost feel … *(Looking at his face.)* even just that name, Markie, loose impressions, I feel as if I were on the verge – figures in the mist almost. Well that's fanciful. But your face … I do feel there's something familiar about it. I used to visit you, you said, we would have chats?

SELDEN: Chats and hot cocoa. I kept a package of marshmallows. Special for you.

*There is a moment.*

HELEN: Marshmallows?

SELDEN: I probably gave you more than I should have. But you loved your hot cocoa and your marshmallows. Well, what child doesn't.

*Something happens inside her.*

*She steps back, suddenly, to put a chair between them.*

*Their eyes lock, for a long moment.*

*Then he lunges suddenly forward to close the gap she gasps and starts to scream.*

*In the blackout the TV flares to life:*

*We're watching that dinner party.*

HARLOWE: And I doubt there's a single person in this room who doesn't still owe the good doctor for a visit or two.

*Again laughter, humorous protests etc.*

HENDERSON: Say don't forget the hammering at all hours of the night, that's another thing we owe him for!

*Laughter.*

WEISS: And the concrete trucks!

HARLOWE: *(Joins in the laughter then holds up his hand.)* I think we can permit a man a few eccentric enthusiasms, and if nocturnal hammering

WEISS: And concrete trucks

HARLOWE: and concrete trucks and a small indulgence in end-times hectoring – gently done, gently done – are the hobby of a man as stand-up as our good doctor why I think a neighborhood can indulge that kind of an appetite.

HENDERSON: To Dr. Stockton's Atom Bomb Shelter!

*Abruptly the sound all but mutes to a low rumble although the picture continues.*

*On stage: an AIRMAN in uniform and, from the opposite direction, a NURSE.*

NURSE: Oh, hello, Colonel. How are you feeling?

FORBES: Just fine thank you, Connie.

NURSE: *(Lightly.)* Professionally, I'm delighted – but personally I'll admit the ward isn't the same without you. You can return to our sterling care at any time.

FORBES: Believe me it's tempting. How's Major Gart?

NURSE: *(Smiling.)* Oh that one. Talk about ingratitude – he's busting to get free and cut loose. He'll be glad to see you.

FORBES: Thanks Connie.

*As FORBES 'enters' GART mutes the TV with the remote control.*

GART: The prodigal Colonel. Welcome. Welcome. How about a shot of straight orangeade?

FORBES: How are you feeling Gart?

GART: Are you serious? One more thermometer in my puss and I'm gonna absent myself without leave from this establishment. Well come on, come on – what's it like in the outside world?

FORBES: Just great.

GART: Well, tell me about it! Who'd you see? Talk to any of the guys?

What about the X-20, Forbes? Did you check her over?

*FORBES glances around briefly.*

FORBES: They've got the ship under wraps. And everybody but the President's Cabinet is looking it over.

GART: They find anything? Any answers.

FORBES: If they have, they sure haven't told me.

GART: You go off on a toot did you? You don't look so good.

FORBES: Don't I?

GART: A little hungover maybe. Got another one of those?

*FORBES shifts and staggers very slightly.*

Steady, Colonel. You look like Xavier Cugat directing a rhumba.

FORBES: Something's happened. Something I don't understand.

GART: Go on.

*FORBES unfurls the newspaper he has been carrying under his arm and shoves the headline towards FORBES.*

FORBES: What's this say? Go ahead, tell me. What's it say?

GART: This?

Lieutenant Colonel Forbes – if this is a literacy test or a sanity test I can assure you that I've been checked out by every doctor in this rinky dink excuse for a health spa –

FORBES: Gart! *Don't get wise with me.* What's it say under the picture. Read it.

*GART gives him a look, but complies.*

GART: "Colonel Clegg Forbes and Major Thomas Gart, taken just before their historic space flight ended in mysterious disappearance and crash." This is not a bad picture, either.

FORBES: That's what you see. It's what I see too. Tom, there were three of us in that ship.

*He searches his face for a sign of recognition.*

There was you and me and a Colonel named Harrington.

GART: Harrington.

FORBES: Ed Harrington. He was thirty-six years old. He was my best friend. I'd known him for fifteen years and you'd known him for five. That ship took a crew of three and we were the three.

GART: Forbes … I don't *know* any Ed Harrington.

*A Police LIEUTENANT and a DOCTOR.*

*The LIEUTENANT is fiddling with a garrote.*

DOCTOR: Got everything you need, Lieutenant?

LIEUTENANT: I think so. It all ties together. Turns out Peter Selden had been embezzling from the mother, she discovered it and, well, you know the rest. Is Miss Foley going to be alright?

DOCTOR: I've given her a sedative. She's a very fortunate woman.

LIEUTENANT: I'll say.

*Holds up the garrote.*

He was going to wait until her back was turned. Lucky for her she screamed her head off when she did. The Super was working in an apartment right down the hall.

DOCTOR: Lucky indeed. And did you locate that little girl? Markie?

LIEUTENANT: Right. Markie.

DOCTOR: She's very eager to make contact with her. She said the little girl knew him somehow, and was afraid of him, and she wants her to know he's no longer a danger.

LIEUTENANT: We've asked around all the units in the building. There's no "Markie" here.

DOCTOR: Perhaps she lives somewhere in the neighborhood.

LIEUTENANT: Perhaps *(He bends down to light a cigarette; when we see his face again he has a certain expression.)* this is the imagination: a land without limits, a map whose borders are marked 'here there be dragons'.

*He steps forward slightly, speaks directly to the audience.*

Explorers have struggled through this terrain for centuries, searching for what passes here for gold. Some return in triumph. Others never re-emerge.

We have just witnessed the journey of Helen Foley, a woman saved by an act, however unwitting, of her imagination. In our next expedition, we join the unusual voyage of one Edward Hall, a man whose imagination may well destroy him. So pack your bags and grasp your compass tight as we set forth into –

DOCTOR: Edward who?

*There is a slight pause.*

LIEUTENANT: Edward what?

DOCTOR: Edward the man who ... who what?

LIEUTENANT: *(Has shaken it off.)* Oh, no, as I was saying: no Markie. Perhaps she just imagined it. You'd be surprised where the brain goes. After a while, in my job, you come to think maybe everyone is a little cuckoo. *(Does twirly 'crazy' gesture.)* Say that's strange. *(Holds up cigarette.)* I don't smoke. Haven't for years. My wife'll be furious if she smells this on me, damned if I know how it got in my pocket.

*Crossing the stage: the NURSE whose face we cannot see*

*slowly unraveling the bandages from the apprehensive WOMAN.*

*As that scene fades out, the LITTLE GIRL from the diner, dripping wet, crosses the stage with a damp wooden carrying case.*

*A BIG HEADED ALIEN follows after her, mopping up with a large extra absorbent towel; midway across the stage he stops and turns to the audience.*

BIG HEADED ALIEN: No no, I'm just happy to help.

*Blackout. In the blackout we hear:*

HALL: I don't even know when I went to sleep. But all of a sudden I wasn't home any more.

I was at a carnival. It was crowded, people were all around me, pushing, yelling …

*Sound of a crowd.*

GAMES BARKER: Hey, buddy, c'mere.

DOGS BARKER: Cotton candy!

GAMES BARKER: Hey, buddy C'mon! Hey!

DOGS BARKER: Cotton candy and salty dogs!

GAMES BARKER: Six shots for a dime hit the bull's eye and claim your prize come on come on how's about it ten cents six chances for ten pennies.

DOGS BARKER: Red hots red hots fifteen cents for a pair of red hots!

GIRLIE BARKER: Hurryhurryhurry! Girls Girls Girls!

*The RIDES BARKER might emerge here.*

RIDES BARKER: Ride the Red Revenger!

*The GIRLIE BARKER might emerge now as well?*

GIRLIE BARKER: Hurry on over to see Maja the cat-girl! Maja the cat-girl Gents!

*Lights up very slowly on HALL, barely lit in the gloom looking all around him in a daze; there is an underlying music while disembodied voices call out from all sides.*

RIDES BARKER: The Red Revenger! The Coaster with the Moster half a mile of unadulterated thrills! Chills! Heights! And Spills!

*The roller coaster has been unleashed, draws ever closer but it is overcome by:*

GIRLIE BARKER: The most exotic and volcanic examples of feminine pulchritude this side of heaven! You like 'em fat? We got 'em! You like 'em slim? Got 'em! Blondes, brunettes, redheads! If they ain't here, believe me, they ain't worth looking at!

And the most exotic and volcanic of them all, the queen of the pride, the pinnacle of the pack –

Come on out of there baby and let them see what you look like – we know you're modest but, we can't expect the good folks here to take my word on this now can we?

*Record plays a Twenties version of 'Caravan'.*

And here she comes …

*Men whistle and roar.*

Maja … *the cat girl!*

*Sailors clapping.*

*Music grows wilder and louder.*

HALL: I didn't know who the girl was, never seen her before, but it almost seemed to me that her eyes were searching the crowd searching … until they found me.

And when they found me

35

I knew I had to get away

Something about those eyes … something deep inside those dark cat's eyes …

*The crowd sounds have died away, oddly submerged, a music begins to thrum itself free.*

*MAJA emerges from the depth of the shadows behind him.*

*She has a walk.*

MAJA: Why did you turn away.

*He doesn't turn around*

Why did you turn and walk away. You were the only one. In the crowd. The only one I noticed.

HALL: I guess I felt like it.

MAJA: Didn't you find me, nice, to look at?

*He turns to her for the first time.*

HALL: Maybe too nice. Aren't you supposed to be back there? Entertaining the customers?

MAJA: I'm free. Free for the night. Are you alone?

HALL: Yes.

MAJA: Then come with me. You do want to, don't you Edward?

HALL: How did you know my name?

MAJA: Oh I know … *lots* of things. Don't be afraid.

HALL: I'm not.

MAJA: Of course not. Come with me. Come.

*She grasps his hands and tugs at him. He stands, immobile.*

You *are* afraid.

HALL: Only because … this isn't happening. I'm not here, I'm at home, in bed, asleep, and you're part of a dream.

MAJA: Well. Why be afraid of a dream.

HALL: I'm only afraid that the dream doesn't *know* it's a dream.

MAJA: Oh I know I'm a dream alright. Come.

*Sounds of a fun house rising: mechanical laughter, artificial ghost sounds, artificial scream, real screams and giggles, a wolf howls? Chains clank. A mechanical dog barks maniacally. Everything tinny, and almost hilarious.*

MAJA: Take me in there, Edward.

HALL: It's for kids.

MAJA: But it's dark in there. Soft and cool and dark.

*She takes his hand.*

HALL: How can I argue with a dream.

*They have entered the fun house. Lots of interesting vivid sounds: a laugher which is not mechanical, a laughter which is not quite human, a ghost moan which is fairly persuasive, a scream which is hilarious, screams which are urgent, chains rattle close by a curtain flaps and flaps a wind rises leaves rustle water drips into a cavern … etc …*

*and in the middle of it all, faint but distinct: a dog barking.*

MAJA: We've been waiting for you, for such a long time.

HALL: *(Startled.)* What?

MAJA: *(She distracts him.)* And now, now you can kiss me.

HALL: Can I. And what if I don't want to.

MAJA: This body, these lips: you want to.

HALL: Look, whose dream is this anyway?

*A series of intense sounds – he sees something which frightens him, and he turns away.*

*MAJA laughs.*

*Something else presumably lunges towards him – with very interesting sounds – really it's all a festival of aural horror – the early 'fun house' assortment of sounds transmuted into something very vivid and real –*

*There's a terrible werewolfy snarfing in there somewhere.*

*Running through it all: something larger and cosmic: something disturbing and shifting and unsettlingly pristine.*

*Running through it all: the coaster: growling, growing closer, the horrible snarfling mechanics of it, the unleashed beast of it.*

*We should hear these sounds in the auditorium as well, from locations from which we have never heard sounds before …*

*He shrinks back, gasping with startlement and fright*

*The coaster roars past*

*The lights black out*

*In the dark:*

*MAJA laughs and laughs.*

HALL: *(We hear but do not see him.)* That's when I knew. I knew she was trying to –

RATHMANN: *(Same.)* And then you woke up.

*Sounds shut out. Lights up on HALL, alone in a chair on an empty stage. Bright daylight.*

HALL: *(Flesh.)* And then I woke up. Gasping. Sweating. My heart beating a mile a minute. Pounding. Pounding. My chest heaving. I lay there absolutely still for an hour until it finally settled down.

I stayed awake until morning and then I got up, went to work. That night I put off sleeping until one o'clock. It didn't matter.

RATHMANN/MAJA: And tell me what happened next, Mr. Hall.

*The Carnival.*

*Roller coaster sounds emerge beneath it.*

HALL: Oh no. No.

*She appears.*

MAJA: Edward, aren't you glad to see me?

HALL: Maja. Please. Have mercy on me. I can't take all of this … excitement …

MAJA: There isn't any excitement, Edward, you said so yourself. You're at home. In bed. Asleep. Aren't you?

HALL: Yes. Yes I am, but –

MAJA: With your blanket pulled up to your chin.

The night light on.

You're perfectly safe.

Edward now is the time to do all of the things you can't do when you're awake.

HALL: Maja that isn't true – my heart –

MAJA: You're free now.

HALL: Maja, that isn't true, the doctor –

*She begins to sing.*

*The roller coaster is drawing near …*

MAJA: Never be afraid …

HALF OF THE BARKERS: to dream

MAJA: Dream everything you want …

OTHER HALF OF THE BARKERS: to do

MAJA: Your dreams are only dreams
They can never injure you

39

BARKERS: Our thoughts can never harm us
Indulge every reverie
We can wander through the mazes
of our mind delightedly

MAJA: Never be afraid to dream
there is safety in our brains
you must trust your every instinct
you must throw aside the chains

BARKERS: of crushing rationality
and seize the fire-y reins
of fantasy and fictions
freedom pulses through your veins

MAJA: Drink the waters that you thirst for
Devour the flame for which you long
In the palace of your dreams
Nothing you do is wrong

*(other voices have joined in:)*

MAJA AND BARKERS: Live your life like it's a dream
When we are dreaming we are free
Your dreams are only dreams
Never fear catastrophe

> *Running through all of this the clack clack clack of the coaster as it leaves the gate and picks up steam and takes a few minor turns and loops and then the slow steady agonizing clack as it hits the final amazing peak before the terrifying plunge.*

> *MAJA hits a high note which is not unlike a pantomime of terror.*

> *EDWARD clutches at his heart.*

> *We are plunged into darkness.*

> *In the darkness:*

GART: What do I remember?

FORBES: What do *you* remember about the flight?

GART: I remember you and me – we've been over this Forbes, we went over this a hundred times. We take off. We black out. Twenty-four hours later, we crash into the desert. That's all I remember!

FORBES: You and me, Gart. You and me.

GART: That's right.

FORBES: Tom there were *three* of us in the X-20. There was you and me and a Colonel named Harrington.

GART: Harrington.

FORBES: Ed Harrington. They discharged Harrington and me yesterday afternoon. We went out to paint the town red.

GART: Forbes … I think you'd better get them to take a look at you.

FORBES: Oh … god.

GART: You look lousy.

FORBES: I'm alright I'm just … just going to get some air …

*Presumably he runs from the room.*

GART: Forbes!

*GART bursts onto the stage in a hospital gown on crutches.*

Forbes!

Somebody get him. Somebody get him, somebody.

*The same NURSE appears.*

NURSE: Did you want something? You should be back in bed Major. If the Doctor saw you on your feet –

GART: You've got to get him back. Colonel Forbes, somebody's got to help him!

NURSE: Who?

GART: Colonel Forbes! He must have rushed right past you.

NURSE: Major, I don't know any Colonel Forbes.

GART: Sure you do Connie you've been slinging him jello and aspirin all week.

Colonel Forbes! Colonel William Forbes!

NURSE: Major let me help you back into bed. I'll call the doctor.

GART: Noooooo …

*He hobbles offstage, pursued by the NURSE.*

*The jingle of a bell as a door opens.*

*A figure in a trenchcoat.*

*We are in the diner.*

HALEY: Something for you?

ROSS: Coffee. Black.

HALEY: One coffee, black. Say, didn't you – what I mean is, didn't you go out on that bus?

ROSS: I did indeed. And you know something? That bridge *wasn't* safe.

HALEY: It wasn't?

ROSS: Not at all. It collapsed.

HALEY: Say, that's terrible!

ROSS: A terrible event indeed. No one survived the long drop into the icy river.

Kersplik.

HALEY: Except you.

ROSS: Except me. Lucky, I guess, huh?

HALEY: Very lucky. But, but –

ROSS: But what?

HALEY: But you're not even wet.

ROSS: Oh … that. An illusion, is all. Like that:

*From the jukebox we hear:*

GREG: Where am I? Oh my God, Phil, *where am I?*

*HALEY gapes.*

*The phone rings.*

*And rings.*

ROSS: Hadn't you better get that?

*Phone keeps ringing. Somehow it sounds even louder.*

*HALEY looks at it apprehensively, then finally picks it up.*

*We hear what he hears: a woman's voice, quite possibly MAJA's*

WOMAN'S VOICE: *(Seductively.)* And this … this is an illusion too *(The voice slowly transitions into ROSS's.)* nothing more than a parlor trick.

*HALEY drops the phone with a cry.*

*We hear a disconnect buzz,*

*Then maybe some other odd noise, maybe like an old-fashioned modem, then it cuts out.*

HALEY: What are you, some kind of a magician?

ROSS: Who, me? Oh, hardly.

*He lights himself a cigarette – ideally Oasis menthols – in the process employing a third arm which emerges from underneath his greatcoat.*

I don't think I need to explain that my name isn't really Ross, and that I'm not really going to Boston. Not yet at least.

HALEY: *(Half wonderment, half something else.)* You don't say.

ROSS: This is a real find, this world. I couldn't be more pleased. Idiots, every one of you, with brains as easy to toy with as a bowl full of spaghetti. *(To the audience.)* Throw a bogeyman or two your way and you fall into line like ducklings in a row. *(Back to HALEY.)* And these *(Airily indicating the cigarette.)* are wonderful. We haven't got a thing like these where I come from. There's going to be a real demand for them, when my friends arrive. I hope you enjoy the agricultural life, Mr. Haley. Well, if you don't, you probably won't have to suffer it for long …

In the meantime, perhaps another cup of coffee while we wait. And maybe a little more of your music.

*He snaps his finger.*

*Jukebox starts up with a perfectly appropriate period tune.*

HALEY: I don't mind. I have a little waiting to do myself. You see, Mr. Ross, my name isn't really Haley.

ROSS: *(Bored.)* Isn't it.

HALEY: It is an extraordinary world, I agree: undeveloped, out of the way, placid sweet-tempered inhabitants with good mouth feel and just the right proportion of chewiness-to-crunch. I can't agree with you about the cigarettes I'm afraid – abominable reeking objects and one of the first things we're going to do when we settle in is outlaw them outright – your friends will be disappointed I know; just as well that they've been delayed … well maybe 'delayed' is putting it a little delicately …

*He snaps his finger. Music on jukebox switches to something very elaborately sci-fi and theremin-ridden.*

by *my* friends.

*Crazy happening. "ROSS" recoils in terror.*

*Lights return to RUTH, GREG, PHIL.*

*All standing around the empty child's bed.*

*We hear the dog barking, from somewhere in the far end of the theater.*

PHIL: And the dog's there as well.

GREG: Mack was barking and barking at the door to the room. We let him in so he wouldn't wake the neighborhood and he just and he just –

he just disappeared.

PHIL: He disappeared. Where? Where did he disappear?

RUTH: The bed. He ran straight at the bed and then he …

*There is a micromoment.*

PHIL: *(With perhaps slightly exaggerated calm.)* Ruth, I'm going to ask you to stay just right where you are. Don't move. Don't move an inch.

Greg –

*He indicates the bed and the two of them shift it.*

Careful. Careful.

*Half crouching, he begins to move exploring the area where the bed was standing, carefully probing the air in front of him with his hands.*

*After a moment:*

GREG: Phil. What are you looking for?

PHIL: I wish I knew for sure.

*More probing.*

TINA: Maaaamaaaaa!

*It is as if she is right there. PHIL freezes in shock. Then recovers, continues probing.*

RUTH: *(Struggling to keep her composure; brightly.)* I'm here baby – I'm right here!

TINA: *(Sleepy.)* Mama I want a glass of water.

RUTH: *(Same.)* I'll get you one baby, just a moment!

*RUTH starts to break down.*

PHIL: Shhhh, Ruthie shhhhh. Stay calm.

She can't hear fear in your voice or she may panic and if she panics she may behave unpredictably or, move. It's crucial that she stays right where she is.

GREG: Where she is.

PHIL: Wherever it is.

RUTH: *(Struggling to speak calmly through near sobs.)* Phil. Where is that.

PHIL: Stay right where you are.

*RUTH presses her hands to her face to keep from crying out.*

*PHIL continues.*

*More poking and prodding at the air.*

*Nothing … nothing.*

*RUTH utters a little sob of despair.*

*There is a tiny frissiony 'zot' noise.*

Ahhhhhhh.

*Using his fingers, very delicately, with light touches which result in small scatters of frissiony sound, PHIL outlines, in the air, a hole a few feet in diameter – during the course of this he accidentally inserts a finger slightly and there's a small shower of sharp sound – he withdraws it hastily.*

The opening.

*With a small cry, RUTH moves towards the opening; PHIL holds her back*

We don't know what's in there.

RUTH: *My daughter is in there.*

PHIL: I know that Ruth, but we can't.

GREG: All we have to do is reach in and pull her out.

PHIL: I don't think it's that simple. If it is – why hasn't Mack found her yet?

*A moment.*

GREG: *(Calling vigorously.)* Mack! Mack!

*We hear a responding bark – from some entire other part of the theater –*

TINA: *(Sleepy.)* Daddy. Daddy I'm *thirsty.*

*We hear her, very distinctly, from another location, slightly cranky and sleep clotted.*

*We hear Mack barking from somewhere else entirely.*

GREG: What … ?

PHIL: If this is another dimension.

And that's the best guess I've got.

Then it won't be laid out like our world.

She may have rolled over or, reached for her dollie.

*An eruption of cheerful barking and, from that same sonic point:*

TINA: *(Worried.)* Mack?

*Sound of doggie enthusiasm and also low growls and grunts.*

PHIL: He's found her!

*Happy cheerful doggie barks.*

GREG: Oh thank God.

TINA: Mackie NO!

PHIL: Ruthie, tell her to grab hold of the dog.

*Mack is making a variety of cheerful busy noises; TINA is whimpering in terror.*

RUTH: *(Abstracted with concern.)* Tell her to...?

PHIL: Maybe Mack can lead her back.

RUTH: *(Comprehending. Hope is dawning.)* Oh –

PHIL: And Ruth –

*He touches her shoulder.*

Remember. You must be absolutely calm. This is crucial.

RUTH: *(She closes her eyes.)* Yes.

*A sound of friendly snuffling, a jingling of dog tags.*

TINA: *(Terrified.)* Go *away* Mack! Go *away*!

PHIL: The collar.

*She takes a moment to steady herself.*

RUTH: *(Loudly.)* Sweetie ... I want you to grab hold of Mack.

*At the sound of his name, Mack has given an adorable determined bark.*

I want you to grab hold of his collar.

*A cheerful little yip.*

TINA: *(Panic.)* No! No Mama, NO!

PHIL: She's afraid of the dog?

GREG: They're best friends. She's just disoriented.

RUTH: Tina, Mack's just trying to help.

*A cheerful little yip.*

*TINA cries out in horror.*

PHIL: *(In an undertone to GREG.)* We haven't got much time.

GREG: *(The same.)* Before … what?

*PHIL looks grim.*

GREG: Before what?

Sweetie listen to me carefully okay?

*Sound of dog growling enthusiastically in the distance.*

TINA: *(Sobbing.)* I want my Mama! I want my Mama!

RUTH: *(Almost sobbing herself.)* I'm right here baby.

GREG: Phil she's right there.

PHIL: I told you –

RUTH: *(Sobbing.)* We're right *here* baby.

GREG: Tina take my hand.

*He puts his hand into the void, sound of a great deal of electronic crackling, lights change.*

PHIL: Greg don't!

*GREG starts to lunge his whole body towards the hole,*

GREG: *Here*, honey –

*As PHIL and RUTH scream:*

*Instant BLACKOUT:*

*Their screams transform almost instantly into something other.*

*From far away: a little girl crying in a remote and vast and echo-y space filled with sonic lunacy (and maybe slightly redolent of the aurora borealis at the beginning).*

GREG: Where am I? Oh my God, Phil, *where am I?*

*END OF ACT 1.*

# Act Two

*We are in total darkness.*

*We are in a very strange place, aurally, the aurally strangest and most involving place we have been so far.*

*There are cosmic echoes, and also unplaceable noises and furtive rustlings*

*We are also hearing some of the odder Fun House sounds as if from a great distance and filtered through an uncanny prism.*

GREG: *(Maybe in a whisper from right behind us.)* Where am I?

… Phil …

where am I?

*PHIL's voice comes from somewhere quite remote.*

PHIL: Don't move, Greg. Don't move an inch.

GREG: … what did you [say]…?

PHIL: *(Shouting, but from somewhere very far away.)* Greg, don't move! I've got you!

*Again: he's very close to us, honestly, he sounds disoriented; words are sluggish foreign objects to him.*

GREG: can't … move …

*PHIL says something else at some length – it is very far away and although it sounds urgent we cannot make it out.*

GREG: Phil?

*Because it doesn't actually sound like PHIL. At all. The voice, whoever it belongs to, continues on for a while longer but we can't make it out.*

*(As he experiences something odd.)*

oh

*Again a remote droning from PHIL.*

GREG: Yeah, can't … can't ah … *(He's trailing off, in many ways.)*

*The PHIL droning has faded almost entirely into the background – we may also hear a faint RUTH chiming, also almost entirely faded into the background.*

*The sound landscape has been intensifying, and transmogrifying and in some way coming closer and becoming more intimate and we spend a tiny bit of time with this.*

*From somewhere deep within it we do hear an odd skree which cuts through it somehow, although only delicately.*

*It rises and we hear, faintly but distinctly:*

TINA: Daaaaaady! Daaaaaady!

GREG: Tina …

*He can remember the name, though not what it signifies.*

*Then he remembers, and shrieks, though his shriek barely dents the engulfing wave of noise:*

Tiiiiina!

Right here sweetheart.

*The word 'here' probably echoes and skitters all around in an alarming fashion.*

PHIL: *(Faintly but distinctly audible.)* Greg. You've got to hurry.

*'Hurry' is another word which probably goes a bit berserk*

Tell her to take hold of Mack.

*(Mack, Mack Mack etc.)*

GREG: *(More to himself than anything.)* Mack. Mack –

oh

Mack!

*From somewhere in the middle distance comes a terrible howl.*

*And then quite suddenly, right up close, a low and terrible growl.*

… Mack?

*A yelp/yawn/stretch of the sort emitted by something with horrid and dripping fangs, super wearwolfy.*

PHIL: She's got to grab on to Mack.

Or she's lost, Greg.

*The phrase 'lost' takes on a brief and mocking life of its own while at the same time Mack emits another very awful howl.*

*There is a brief period of stretched time.*

GREG: Tina … Mack's collar.

*Another wearwolfy snarfling.*

TINA: No!

GREG: I know he's scary.

I know.

*Some very weird noise. Not Mack-specific but not un-Mack-related.*

GREG: *(Harsh.)* Grab on Tina!

TINA: *(A plea.)* No!

GREG: *(He gathers his forces.)* This is not a request.

*A brief sob/shriek from TINA.*

DO IT.

*There is a moment.*

TINA: *(A sob, a sniffle, a gulp.)* Alright Daddy.

*Meanwhile there are scary Mack snorfles.*

GREG: Are you holding on?

TINA: *(Sad. Scared. Broken.)* … yes …

GREG: Mack. Mack!

*The snorfles cease for a moment, and there is a kind of diabolical mini roar.*

*TINA sobs.*

*We should hear GREG breathing for a moment. Very up close.*

GREG: Come here boy.

*And now the scary Mack noises are coming closer.*

Here boy.

*We can hear GREG's breathing.*

RUTH: *(Faint and far away.)* Come here Mack, come here.

GREG: Here.

*More scary snarfling as he comes closer.*

PHIL: *(Faint and far away but distinct.)* He's doing it. Man, what a mutt.

*As the noises get closer and closer they are more overwhelmingly scary.*

*Amongst them some kinds of noises from TINA.*

GREG: *(Almost a chant in the face of the incoming terror.)* Here Mack, here Mack here Mack here Mack here

*Mack descends with an epic eruption of growls.*

*GREG cries out half in terror, and half in triumph.*

I have her!

PHIL: Hold on as tight as you can!

Now Ruth – tug, tug now!

*Some sort of very extraordinary sound.*

*Mack's howls transform to triumphant barks.*

*Lights on GREG on the floor, RUTH nearby is clutching TINA to her.*

We almost lost you Greg – that gap was closing so fast –
another minute and you would have been trapped over there.

GREG: How did you get me out?

PHIL: We had hold of you the entire time.

GREG: You had hold of me?

PHIL: Half of you was still here. The other half ...

*PHIL has been cupping his hand to light his cigarette.*

GREG: Was where. Where, Phil?

PHIL: *(To the audience.)* A place where the improbable is
possible, the impossible probable; a region as vast as space
and as timeless as infinity a place of shadow and substance
... you crossed over into ... into ... into

GREG: In where, Phil? Into where!

*There is a slight blank pause while PHIL restores, covers.*

Where did I cross into, Phil?

PHIL: Uh, nowhere.

*He sees the cigarette and – rightfully connecting it with the sudden
annoying phenomenon, swiftly and covertly dispatches with it.
Brushes his hands off.*

Duluth, Greg, I don't know.

GREG: Duluth?

*As PHIL brushes himself off, rises, and exits.*

PHIL: Duluth, Kansas City, Witchita, Vegas, Binghamton,
Chicago, Omaha, I don't know and I don't care to know!

*The BANDAGED WOMAN faces us.*

*On either side of her, the NURSE, and a DOCTOR.*

*The NURSE hands the DOCTOR a scissors and with great precision,
and agonizing slowness, he cuts away the remainder of her bandages.*

*She is beautiful.*

*The DOCTOR and the NURSE are terribly still*

*The face of the WOMAN registers great hope and terrible apprehension.*

*Slowly, terribly slowly, the NURSE raises a hand mirror so that the WOMAN can see her reflection.*

*When she does so she breaks into great racking sobs.*

*The NURSE and DOCTOR turn sadly away.*

*Their faces are monstrous.*

*GENERAL WALTERS, on her way out of the building, is intercepted by an aide.*

ADJUNCT: General Walters?

GENERAL WALTERS: Yes?

ADJUNCT: General Walters. We've had contact, Ma'am. It's one of the old jobs Ma'am, spiraling in.

WALTERS: *(Tired.)* Let's hear it.

ADJUNCT: A ship called Solar 2. Commanded by a Douglas Stansfield.

GENERAL WALTERS: *(No file.)* A Douglas Stansfield. And … how long has this one been out there.

ADJUNCT: Fifty-two years, Ma'am. Fifty-two years, three months and *(Briefly calculating.)* twenty-six days.

GENERAL WALTERS: Fifty-two years. This is one of the pioneers. He must be one of the very first. Oh god I hate this part of the job. *(Shaking her head.)* Years and years in space on a mission that was obsolete almost the moment they were out of sight and now they come back. Every year. Every month. They come back. Burnt. Dented. Smashed. Useless. And very much alone. Obsolete misfits. What should have been a man's best years spent fruitlessly. In a tin can in a sparkling void.

ADJUNCT: *(Sees something.)* Hold on. This is a funny one.

GENERAL WALTERS: How's that?

ADJUNCT: In Stansfield's file. There's an insertion from a Bixler –

GENERAL WALTERS: Bixler. You see his name a lot in these old files, that's the busybody who sent most of our castaways up into space in the first place. I'd love to wring his neck. What does ol' Bixler want now.

ADJUNCT: Well you'd better take a look at this sir.

*He passes slip of paper over to GENERAL WALTERS who scans it briefly.*

*As they are exiting the stage:*

GENERAL WALTERS: Well this is curious … damned curious …

*Fifty-two years previous …*

*DR. BIXLER and COMMANDER STANSFIELD.*

BIXLER: This, Commander Stansfield, is a small solar system, much like ours. With a sun, much like ours and planets which run in roughly the same orbital patterns we do around our own sun.

We believe it is possible that this system could support life.

*He pauses for a second to let his next point land:*

Sentient life.

STANSFIELD: Sentient life …

That's where I'm going.

BIXLER: That's where you're going.

STANSFIELD: When?

BIXLER: In about six months. They're building the ship right now.

STANSFIELD: Doctor Bixler I … I like this assignment very much.

BIXLER: Which is precisely why you've been chosen.

There are the usual unknowns, the usual dangers.

STANSFIELD: It was ever thus.

BIXLER: No, Commander, it was *never* thus. Not precisely.

In the past you've contended with meteor storms, space junk, mechanical difficulty and malfunction, calculation and miscalculation, physical exertion, mental endurance – well you'll still have all of those, you'll have them compounded but there's another factor here altogether.

*Several clicks on the little device.*

STANSFIELD: Distance.

BIXLER: Distance indeed. This cluster is at a rough estimate a hundred and forty-one light years away from us.

The ship will have an inter-stellar drive and an anti-gravity device. The fastest man-made object ever conceived and brought to life. Speed never before dreamt of. But in terms of the space you have to conquer – it'll be like an ant crossing the Sahara.

In short, Commander, your trip to these planetary bodies, and then back to earth, will take approximately forty-five to fifty years.

*STANSFIELD lets this sink in a moment.*

STANSFIELD: That's a high mountain Dr. Bixler.

BIXLER: A very high mountain indeed. The highest in the history of mankind. The longest trip in the history of man. You're thirty-one years old, Commander. When you return from this trip … the earth will have aged almost half a century.

STANSFIELD: That's something to contemplate. I'll be over eighty years old.

*He looks away very thoughtfully*

I'll have lived the better part of my life out in space … and alone.

BIXLER: You'll have lived the better part of *a* life, Commander, but as for yours … we intend to try something new. Also a risk. Also decidedly calculated.

STANSFIELD: Cryogenics?

BIXLER: Suspended animation. We have yet to test it on a human subject for any real length of time, but the initial results are promising, promising indeed. The earth will age, Commander, but you will not. You'll be just a few weeks older when you return.

STANSFIELD: It'll be … sort of like dying and then, coming to life again.

BIXLER: But coming to life as a stranger, Commander, I need to make sure you understand that. Returning to human society as a … as a profound anachronism.

It's a lonely assignment, Stansfield and, if you'll forgive this degree of candor, it's one I don't much envy.

STANSFIELD: That's been pretty much the story of my life, Dr. Bixler. Assignments that not very many people would envy – apart from the very odd, the very adventuresome.

*There's a moment's silence.*

Does this system have a name, Dr. Bixler?

BIXLER: We've been calling it Solar 2, for want of another name. But you can call it anything you want.

You can call it, Stansfield's Mount Everest.

A challenge brand-new in human experience. The kind of adventure we don't have on the earth any more, the kind of achievement which is no longer possible here.

*After a moment,* STANSFIELD *grins.*

STANSFIELD: When do I begin?

*As he leads him offstage, with relief and pride:*

BIXLER: You have begun. As of this moment.

*The stage is dark, and bare.*

*The TV kicks in on its own:*

HENDERSON: To Dr. Stockton's Atom Bomb Shelter!

*A few jovial cries of: hear hear! And "to The Shelter!"*

*On the TV:*

*Applause and laughter.*

STOCKTON: *(Grinning.)* You dirty dog, you! First a surprise party
– which I abhor. And then that sloppy sentimental speech!

Well I think you'll have to permit me to get in a few licks of
my own –

LILY: *(Urgently.)* Hey, Pop? Pop?

STOCKTON: What is it Lily?

LILY: The picture went out on the TV set. Then there was a
goofy announcement.

*The child continues to speak but is drowned out by one of the women
laughing.*

*STOCKTON leans down and grips the child's shoulders.*

WEISS: *(With driving urgency.)* Hold it, everybody.

*The laughter swiftly dwindles to silence.*

STOCKTON: Lily, tell me again.

LILY: The announcer said, we should turn to the to the *(Has
trouble pronouncing it.)* Conelad station on the radio.

WEISS: Conelrad.

STOCKTON: Are you sure, Lily?

LILY: I didn't hear it wrong. That's what he said. He said turn on your Conelrad station. Then the TV went all fuzzy.

*The TV signal abruptly terminates, leaving only fuzz.*

*The BARTENDER frowns, reaches up and whacks the side of the TV set, fiddles with a knob.*

*HALL, lapsed into a brown study on one end of the bar, raises a finger and the BARTENDER bends down to listen as he says something too low to catch.*

BARTENDER: You said you wanted to get fortified, Pal. I put everything in there but Atomic Energy –

*FORBES and HARRINGTON enter.*

Say aren't you guys Forbes and Harrington? Aren't you the guys who was up in space?

*Holds up newspaper big picture of three men.*

HARRINGTON: *(To FORBES.)* One time a fortune teller in a carnival in Des Moines said I'd be famous.

FORBES: That and thirty cents should get us a beer a piece shouldn't it?

BARTENDER: You bet your life, but never mind the thirty cents! This is on the house. I don't get many celebrities here. Go ahead boys, drink hearty! I don't even mind you crackin' up the space ship and I'm a tax payer!

*HARRINGTON looks woozy for a moment.*

FORBES: What's the matter?

BARTENDER: Something wrong?

HARRINGTON: I'll tell you after I taste the beer. Happy Landings ... whenever possible

*They clink glasses.*

FORBES: Happy Landings.

*As HARRINGTON is bringing it to his lips, his glass drops and shatters.*

BARTENDER: That's okay. That's okay. That ain't the last glass of beer in the house, let me tell you. I'll get you another one right away Colonel!

FORBES: You sick, Ed?

HARRINGTON: No. No, I'm not sick. I just got this ... funny feeling.

FORBES: What kind of feeling?

HARRINGTON: Hard to explain.

*The BARTENDER slides another glass of beer across the counter and HARRINGTON lifts it:*

Happy Landings.

*He quaffs a long draught.*

I'm gonna call my folks.

FORBES: Ed, you alright?

HARRINGTON: Yeah, I'm alright.

*HARRINGTON exits abruptly.*

FORBES: Sorry about that.

BARTENDER: Aw, ferget it!

*A LITTLE GIRL marches up to the bar. Sits on a stool. Sits her wooden case on the seat next to her and from it she pulls her VENTRILOQUIST DUMMY and sits him next to her.*

LITTLE GIRL: I'd like a shot of whiskey, straight up.

BARTENDER: Little girl, we don't serve little girls.

LITTLE GIRL: Oh it isn't for me. It's for Napoleon, here.

BARTENDER: Well we don't serve dolls, neither.

LITTLE GIRL: Napoleon isn't a doll. He's a dummy.

*DUMMY turns his head towards her.*

Only in the technical sense.

DUMMY: Let me do the talking, sweetheart.

I'd like a shot of whiskey, straight up.

BARTENDER: A shot of whiskey, eh.

DUMMY: Straight up. Better make it a double.

*BARTENDER peers over the bar, as if looking for an accomplice.*

BARTENDER: *(Impressed.)* You doing all that by yourself Honey?

DUMMY: Yes yes. She's a rare talent. Whiskey!

BARTENDER: You got yourself a real good act there.

You tell jokes or anything like that?

DUMMY: Shall we strike a bargain? We will tell you a joke you will provide me with a whiskey. A double. Deal?

BARTENDER: Alright – you got yourself a deal.

*DUMMY turns to look at her.*

DUMMY: Take it away Sweetie.

LITTLE GIRL: *(Clears her throat and then proceeds with professional poise.)* Napoleon.

Which earth custom do Alien visitors find the most humorous?

DUMMY: *(Crisply.)* Beauty contests. *(To BARTENDER.)* Alright?

BARTENDER: *(Pondering it.)* Beauty contests …

LITTLE GIRL: Because the aliens think that we are/

DUMMY: Unspeakably

LITTLE GIRL: Ugly/all of us

DUMMY: Hideous

BARTENDER: Yeah that joke I don't know about.

DUMMY: Alright.

Hit it:

LITTLE GIRL: Napoleon, you look frazzled.

DUMMY: Oh I am sweetheart, I am. This morning, I find my wife staring at a bottle of orange juice.

LITTLE GIRL: Why was she doing that?

DUMMY: I ask her. "Because it says: concentrate".

*A tiny beat; he gets it.*

BARTENDER: Now you're cooking! That's the stuff!

DUMMY: A deal, as I must remind you, is a deal.

BARTENDER: Sure thing *(Pouring.)* and I'll tell you what – you want to come by tonight, say around 9:30. We always have a little crowd.

*The GIRL is pouring whiskey into the DUMMY's open mouth.*

DUMMY: It's hard to say where our travels may take us but it is possible we will grace your establishment tonight.

In the meantime, Sweetheart, take me away from this hell hole.

BARTENDER: Ha ha ha, hell hole, that's the stuff, that's the stuff.

*MAJA enters the bar.*

*HALL flees the bar.*

*HARRINGTON returns.*

HARRINGTON: Forbes.

FORBES: What's the trouble Harrington, you look awful.

63

HARRINGTON: I just called home. Just called my folks. My mother answered. I told her it was me. And she said … she said she didn't have any son named Ed Harrington. That's what she said, Forbes. And I asked to talk to the Old Man and when he got on he kept saying for me to hang up. He didn't want any practical jokers bothering his wife. Forbes, he said he didn't have any son at all what is this what's going on?

FORBES: A gag maybe, or …

HARRINGTON: My folks? You're kidding me. This is no gag, Forbes.

FORBES: And you're sure you got the right number?

HARRINGTON: Think I don't know my own mother? My own father? No, this is part, part of that feeling …

FORBES: What feeling?

HARRINGTON: The feeling … I don't know. The feeling something's not right. Things aren't what they're supposed to be. Something's opened up we opened something up somehow something we don't know how to shut –

FORBES: Ed what you need is a good stiff drink.

HARRINGTON: Sure. Sure it couldn't hurt could it. I'll be right back Forbes. I'm going to go splash water on my face.

FORBES: Bartender, get me a whiskey for my friend, actually, better make it a double. And one for me too please. Actually, make it a double too!

BARTENDER: Two doubles. I make that: a quadruple. I don't usually like to serve a quadruple; this isn't that kind of joint, but seeing as you're a space hero I'm willing to make an exception.

*Pours a big glass of whiskey and serves.*

FORBES: What? No. I asked for two doubles. One for me and one for my buddy.

BARTENDER: One for your "buddy" eh? Well if that's the way you like it, why not.

*Pours half into another glass.*

One for you. One for your "buddy".

FORBES: Yes. My buddy. Colonel Harrington. Who was just here with me. *(Aggressively.)* You know Colonel Harrington.

BARTENDER: Colonel with all due respect I never met the guy.

FORBES: Colonel Harrington. We came in together. You served him a beer he dropped it on the floor –

*He picks up the newspaper and shoves it in his face.*

– you remember Colonel Harrington.

BARTENDER: That guy on the left? I never saw that guy

FORBES: Gart is on the left Harrington –

*He is looking at the headline – we can see it too – there are only two figures in the photograph.*

Harrington.

*Drops the paper and runs offstage. Door, echoey sound as if he's in the bathroom.*

Harrington!

Harrington.

*He returns, runs out the front door.*

*A loudspeaker announcement:*

LOUDSPEAKER: Will communications team B-8 … communications team B-8 report to Central Control. Communications team B-8 to Central Control.

*Two UNIFORMED MEN walk hurriedly across the stage, followed by a YOUNG WOMAN in a professional looking smock.*

*She drops a sheaf of papers she's been carrying and they drift to the floor, scattering all over.*

*She drops to her knees and begins picking them up. Almost immediately STANSFIELD, who has just arrived on the scene, drops down beside her to assist.*

SANDY: A friend in need.

STANSFIELD: That's my job.

SANDY: Picking up papers?

STANSFIELD: I'm the new morale officer. I follow people around who look stricken.

*Smiling, she takes the papers from his hand, rises.*

SANDY: Do I look stricken?

STANSFIELD: Momentarily nonplussed.

*He looks at her for a moment.*

STANSFIELD: I don't think we've met. You permanently stationed here?

SANDY: I'm with NASA, on detached duty. And you're – ?

STANSFIELD: Stansfield. Commander U.S.N.

SANDY: Why, you're the –

you're the one.

STANSFIELD: *(Grinning.)* I don't know whether to thank you for that one, or report you for insubordination.

*They laugh.*

SANDY: Forgive me. We've been hearing "Stansfield, Stansfield, Stansfield" for close to a year. I've so wanted to meet you.

STANSFIELD: And I, have so wanted to meet you.

*SANDY starts to protest.*

66

It's true. I've got E.S.P. One morning, a long time ago, I woke up to an inner voice which told me, with some intensity, that I'd meet a girl with a stricken look who drops papers in corridors.

SANDY: Did your E.S.P. give you the name?

STANSFIELD: Sandra. Sandra Horn.

*She gapes at him for a moment and then, laughing, touches her name plate.*

SANDY: The subtle astronaut.

*They share a laugh.*

It's been an honor meeting you.

*Rather compulsively, she extends her hand.*

*He takes it. They shake.*

*There is a moment.*

*Where they don't quite let go of each other's hand.*

*The moment extends a moment past that.*

*They release each other's hands*

STANSFIELD: *(Finally.)* I don't suppose … I don't suppose the National Space Agency could do without your services for say, a couple of hours this evening? Long enough for a dinner?

SANDY: I think … despite the fact that I'm invaluable and the whole space program rests on me alone –

a two or three hour period might be carved out. I'm in the book, Commander.

*A bit of a beat. Lightly.*

Please phone me.

STANSFIELD: I won't call – I'll pick up. I'll be there at eight. What kind of food do you like?

SANDY: Any kind. Partial to beef. Like seafood. Chinese, Italian – you name it.

STANSFIELD: I'll plan the itinerary and the menu. See you at eight. Arrivederci, lady from the Space Agency.

SANDY: *(Smiling at him but with a note of wonder in her eyes.)* At eight o'clock … astronaut … arrivederci.

*They exit in their separate directions.*

*The sound of reality being sucked back into position.*

*Lights up.*

*We're in the psychiatrist's office.*

RATHMANN: And is that it?

HALL: That's it. If I go to sleep, I'm right back there with her the coaster the – and that will be the end of me.

On the other hand, if I stay awake much longer the strain will be too much for my heart and *that'll* be the end of me. Heads I lose, tails I lose. Quite a choice, isn't it.

*There is a violent pounding, at the door.*

HALL: Oh my god. What was that?

*RATHMANN looks nonplussed.*

*HALL is rigid with terror.*

HALL: That – didn't you hear that?

RATHMANN: Hear *what* Mr. Hall?

HALL: The door …

*RATHMANN looks at the door.*

*As if on cue there is a very light tapping.*

RATHMANN: That's probably Miss Williams, my secretary.

*Calling out:*

Miss Williams, I'm in a *session.*

*With a perhaps exaggerated creaking the door cracks open and a woman in impeccably respectable secretarial tweeds, horn rimmed glasses etc. peeks through.*

*She is played by the actress who plays MAJA.*

*It's worth noting that by this point the lighting should have become imperceptibly but distinctly shadowy and mildly sinister.*

MAJA THE SECRETARY: Dr. Rathmann I'm *so sorry* to disturb you but –

*HALL utters a mad shriek and sits bolt upright.*

*LIGHTS OUT: Sound?*

*Something.*

*Lights restore mere seconds later: bright and full and normal: a sunlit office.*

*HALL is slumped in the chair; RATHMANN, bent over him, is taking his pulse.*

*The SECRETARY is now in the room.*

MAJA THE SECRETARY: Dr. Rathmann?

RATHMANN: *(Looking up.)* I'm afraid he's dead.

MAJA THE SECRETARY: Dead?

RATHMANN: I'm afraid so.

MAJA THE SECRETARY: But he came in just a minute ago!

RATHMANN: *(A little dazed.)* He came in just a minute ago. I had just introduced myself, we had just *(He indicates the chairs.)* and then he, in perhaps two seconds, he was asleep. Fast asleep.

I was just about to shake him awake when you knocked and he, he just slumped over …

MAJA THE SECRETARY:What is it is it a heart attack?

RATHMANN: Probably

MAJA THE SECRETARY: A heart … *attack* …

RATHMANN: I suppose there are worse ways to go. At least he died peacefully.

MAJA THE SECRETARY: Peacefully. We all of us yearn for a peaceful death, a peaceful life. But it must be said that we live *peacefully*, at our peril.

*She has stepped forward, and is addressing the audience.*

In our dreams we live the incredible, the forbidden; we approach the impossible. But what becomes of the man or woman who does not taste some small measure of these bewitching tonics in waking life? Must we not all at least sip at madness, at the amazing?

And if we do not … will not madness and the amazing sip … at the bewitching tonic of ourselves?

RATHMANN: Miss Williams?

MAJA THE SECRETARY: Tonight's refreshment comes to you straight from the soda fountains of …

RATHMANN: Miss Williams!

*A blank pause for a moment and then she shakes herself clear.*

MAJA THE SECRETARY: Yes, Dr. Rathmann?

RATHMANN: You were – what was that, you were saying?

MAJA THE SECRETARY: *(Still a bit pulling herself out from a daze.)* I was saying, I was saying – I was saying what will I tell your next patient, Miss Sturka? She's in the waiting room and how will we, how will we remove this body without alarming everyone and also, Dr. Rathman, why –

*Her pockets are crammed with cigarettes:*

Oh god.

*The soundscape shifts to the mechanisms of a docking bay: machineries, small sirens.*

ALL BUT MECHANICAL FEMALE VOICE: Nine minutes to countdown, nine minutes

*STANSFIELD approaches, fully suited, and as he does SANDY steps forward, as she does so the soundscape mutes almost entirely; just a faint dim ringing in the background, curiously muffled; perhaps there is music?*

SANDY: Commander Stansfield?

*He sees her, stops.*

A small unofficial gesture from one of the lesser bureaucrats of our good gray respectable government.

*She reaches up, kisses him, a kiss he passionately returns.*

*They break and stand holding tight onto each other's hands.*

Unofficial ... and very much apart from protocol. But I couldn't let you leave, Doug ... not without saying goodbye. Not without telling you that ...

that I have loved you very much, these few months. That I shall sorely miss you. That my life ... all the rest of it ... will be a strangely meaningless, dull and empty thing without you to share it.

ALL BUT MECHANICAL FEMALE VOICE: Eight minutes to Countdown, eight minutes.

*He starts to say something; she puts a finger to his lips.*

SANDY: And this last paragraph. I wouldn't say this to you if I didn't know the kind of man you are. I wouldn't say any of this. But I know you. I know you're built out of a very strong alloy and you may bend a little ... but you'll never break.

*He touches his hand to her cheek.*

STANSFIELD: *(Very softly.)* It's a very odd thing, Sandy. A very odd thing. I've moved forward, my entire life. I've never looked back.

SANDY: I know that.

STANSFIELD: My life has been space. It's been missions, projects, and expeditions. I haven't had the time for intrusions. I haven't had the patience for … mysteries. But this.

*He cups her face.*

This is a mystery I would have had the patience for. All the patience in the universe.

And when I return. When I touch this ground again. The first thought I'll have, the first thing I'll want to see. The first … touch …

SANDY: I'll be the little old lady in the lace shawl. The one waving the "welcome home" sign. So look for me, Doug, will you? Look for me on the fringe. I'll be … I'll be carrying the sign.

*She turns abruptly and walks away from him. He stands there a moment, staring after her.*

ALL BUT MECHANICAL FEMALE VOICE: Seven minutes to Countdown, seven minutes.

*And half cutting across that announcement, less recorded and stately another female voice:*

ACTUAL AND HASTY FEMALE VOICE: Commander Stansfield please report to Launch Gate 4. Commander Stansfield, you're expected at Launch Gate 4.

*There is a microbeat and then he shakes himself out of something and heads off in the opposite direction.*

*The stage plunges into darkness. An air raid siren.*

*The TV flares to life.*

*As it broadcasts, the cast gathers around it in the dim.*

THE TV: ... direct from Washington DC. Repeating that. This is Conelrad. This is Conelrad. Four minutes ago the President of the United States made the following announcement. I quote: "At 11:04 PM Eastern Standard Time both our Distant Early Warning line and Ballistics Early Warning Line reported radar evidence of missiles flying due south east. As of this moment, the nature of these objects is undetermined but for the time being, and in the interest of national safety we are declaring a state of Yellow Alert.

The Civil Defense authorities request that if you have a shelter already prepared go there at once. If you do not have a shelter use your time to move supplies of food, water, medicine and other supplies to a central place. Keep all doors and windows closed. Please stay tuned to this channel for further updates.

*Great clatter as party exits all at once.*

*The door to the shelter, a trap in the center of the room, opens, light diffusing upward.*

*LILY enters with a lemonade jug and an ornamental vase, both full of water.*

GRACE: *(From off.)* There's hardly any water coming through the tap.

STOCKTON: That's because everybody and his brother is doing the same thing we are. Keep it on full force until it stops. Fill as many as you can. Careful, Lily, careful, put them on the table.

*LILY descends carefully.*

*The lights dim for a moment.*

I'm going to start up the generator for when the power goes off. Could happen at any moment.

*As he starts down from the kitchen offstage there is a crash from offstage and an inarticulate cry.*

73

*He steps back up.*

Grace?

GRACE: I'm alright, I'm alright. I just, the jug slipped.

STOCKTON: *(Gentle but firm.)* Easy Gracie, easy. Make believe it's perfume and it costs a hundred bucks an ounce. Maybe in an hour or so it'll cost even more than that –

LILY: *(Up from basement.)* What else, pop?

STOCKTON: All the canned goods down?

LILY: All that I could find.

GRACE: How about the fruit cellar?

LILY: I put all those in too.

STOCKTON: Get my bag from the bedroom. Put that in there too.

LILY: What about books and stuff?

GRACE: *(Close to hysteria.)* Your father told you to get his bag!

STOCKTON: There's time, Grace. There's plenty of time. And we'll need books. Who knows how long we'll have to stay down there.

LILY: I'll get your bag Pop.

STOCKTON: What about lightbulbs. Where do you keep the light bulbs?

GRACE: Top shelf in the utility closet.

*Then closes her eyes tightly and clenching her fists.*

We don't have any. I ran out yesterday. I was going to buy some at the store. There was a sale on –

*She lets out a sob.*

– how much time do we have

74

STOCKTON: Seems to me I remember reading someplace from the first alarm we might have anywhere from fifteen minutes to half an hour.

GRACE: *(Eyes going wide.)* Fifteen minutes!

STOCKTON: I'm winging it, Honey. I don't know for sure. I don't think anyone does.

*He heads towards the door.*

Keep an eye on the water!

GRACE: Where are you going!?

*As he descends he goes to GRACE, takes her hands in his.*

STOCKTON: There's no guarantee this lands near us.

GRACE: *(Interrupting, pulling her hands away.)* But if it does – we're forty miles from New York. And New York's going to get it. We know that. And then we'll get it too. All of it. The poison the radiation the whole thing. We'll get it too.

STOCKTON: We'll be in a shelter, Grace. And with any luck at all, we'll survive. We've got enough food and water to last us two weeks. Maybe even longer, if we use it wisely.

GRACE: And then what? Then what Bill? We crawl out of here like gophers to tip toe through all the rubble up above. The rubble and the ruins and the bodies of our friends.

*She gives him a long queer look, composite of horror and a building panic.*

Why is it so necessary that we survive? What's the good of it Bill?

*She suddenly breaks, grabbing him, her voice a drawn out sob.*

Bill, wouldn't it be better … wouldn't it be quicker and easier if we just –

*LILY enters with the bag and an armful of books and magazines.*

LILY: I got everything Pop.

STOCKTON: Careful with the steps Lily.

*When LILY is out of sight.*

That's why we have to survive. *That's* the reason. She may inherit just rubble now but she's eight years old.

Eight years old, Grace.

*We hear the water slowing from a stream to drips, drips, drips.*

There's a five gallon can of gasoline in the garage, we'll need it for the generator, I'll be right back.

*A knock.*

*JERRY HARLOWE enters.*

HARLOWE: How you doing Bill?

STOCKTON: Collecting water which is what you should be doing.

HARLOWE: We got about thirty gallons and the water stopped. Did yours stop too?

STOCKTON: *(Nods.)* You better get on home, Jerry. Get into your shel –

*He stops abruptly, wets his lips.*

Into your basement. I'd board up the windows if I were you. And if you've got any wood putty or anything I'd seal the corners.

LILY: Anything else pop?

STOCKTON: The last jar of water Lily, careful.

*She slowly and carefully descends the stairs. When she is out of sight.*

HARLOWE: *(His voice is very gentle.)* We don't have a cellar, Bill. Remember?

*(Then a lopsided grin.)* The benefits of modern architecture. We've got the one brand-new house on the street. Everything at your beck and call. Everything at your fingertips. And a nice electrical laundry room right off the kitchen.

*(His voice shakes slightly.)* Every wonder of modern science taken into account except the one that's heading for us now.

*Silence. HARLOWE tries to keep supplication out of his voice.*

Bill, can I bring Martha and the kids over here?

STOCKTON: Over *here?*

HARLOWE: We're sitting ducks over there. Sitting ducks. We don't have any protection at all.

STOCKTON: *(After a moment's hesitation.)* You can use our basement.

HARLOWE: Your basement? What about your shelter? That's the only place anyone can survive! We've got to get into a shelter.

*A beat.*

STOCKTON: I don't have any room, Jerry. I don't have near enough room. Or supplies or anything. It's designed for three people.

HARLOWE: We'll bring our own water, and our own food. We'll sleep on top of one another if necessary. Please ... Bill. We've got to use your shelter. I've got to keep my family alive. We won't use any of your stuff.

STOCKTON: What about air? Will you bring your own air? That's a ten by ten room, Jerry.

HARLOWE: *(Momentarily taken aback and having to recover.)* Just let us stay in there the first forty-eight hours or so, then we'll get out. Just so we have a chance during the rough time.

STOCKTON: When that door gets closed and locked – it *stays* closed and locked. There'll be radiation and heaven knows what else.

*And now his face is torn by anguish.*

I'm sorry, Jerry. As God is my witness, I'm sorry. But I built that for *my* family.

HARLOWE: *(Grabbing him, his voice high, shrill, and unsteady.)* What about *mine?* What do *we* do? Rock on the front porch until we burn into cinders?

STOCKTON: At this moment it's *my* family I have to worry about.

*He starts towards the door.*

HARLOWE: I'm not going to sit by and watch my wife and children die in agony. I'm not going to do that. Do you understand me, Bill?

*He shakes STOCKTON.*

I'm not going to do that!

*STOCKTON drops.*

HARLOWE: I'm sorry, Bill. Please forgive me.

STOCKTON: *(Guiltily averts his eyes and then looks up, in a very soft and gentle voice.)* I kept telling you. All of you. Build a shelter. Get ready. Forget the card parties and the barbeques for maybe two hours a week.

And admit to yourself that the worst is possible.

But you didn't want to listen, Jerry. None of you wanted to listen. To build a shelter was admitting the kind of age we lived in and none of you had the guts to face that. So now, Jerry, now you've got to find some guts to face something far worse. God protect you, Jerry. It's out of my hands now. It's simply out of my hands.

*He turns and goes down the steps to the shelter and shuts the door after him.*

*As HARLOWE stands there, the front door is flung open and in walks MARTY WEISS and his wife with an infant in her arms.*

MARTY WEISS: Bill? Bill?

MRS. WEISS: *(To HARLOWE.)* They're already in the shelter aren't they. *(To her husband.)* I *told you* we waited too long but you *dithered.*

HARLOWE: It's no use, Marty. He isn't letting anyone in.

WEISS: He's got to let us in. We don't even have windows in half the basement. I don't have anything to plug them with, either.

MRS. WEISS: A basement isn't any help anyway.

WEISS: This it?

*Kneeling and pounding on the floor.*

Bill? Bill? It's Marty. We've got Paul with us. Bill?

*The lights go out. Mrs. WEISS screams. In the distance the siren starts up again.*

Bill. Please, Bill, let us in. Let us in Bill, please.

*The lights flicker back on. A beat.*

I feel sorry for you, Bill, I really do. You probably will survive *(Breaking into almost a roar.)* but you'll have blood on your hands. You're a doctor, Bill. You're supposed to help people!

*Mr. MARTIN has arrived.*

MARTIN: It's going to land at any minute isn't it, it's going to land at any minute.

MRS. WEISS: What are we going to do, Marty, what are we going to do?

*The TV flickers to life.*

CONELRAD: This is Conelrad. This is Conelrad. We've been asked to once again remind the population to remain calm, stay off the streets. This is urgent.

*WEISS bangs again, frantic, on the shelter door.*

*HENDERSON emerges from the top of the stairs.*

WEISS: Bill!

Bill!

HARLOWE: *(To HENDERSON.)* Don't waste your time. He won't let anyone in.

MRS. WEISS: We've got to do *something*.

HARLOWE: Maybe we ought to pick out just one basement and go to work on it. Pool all our stuff. Food, water, everything.

MRS. MARTIN: That's great. And that's just wonderful. Let's nail boards to the windows and, hang sheets and maybe we have some strips of tin foil we can use. Let's do everything we can in the next ten minutes and then, and then we can just huddle together, and we can watch, while our kids, while our kids …

MARTY WEISS: Maybe we should try to break open the door.

*There are voices of assent.*

HARLOWE: Wait a minute. Wait a minute. Think. All of us couldn't fit in there. It would be crazy to even try.

HENDERSON: If it saves even one of our kids –

MARTY WEISS: Why don't we draw lots? Pick out one family?

*Agreement.*

HARLOWE: I'm telling you he's not going to agree to that.

MARTIN: We can make him agree to it. We can't all fit in there but we can make him agree to it. When he sees the whole street is against him?

*Agreement.*

*MARTIN straddles the trap.*

Bill? Bill Stockton? You've got a bunch of your neighbors here who want to stay alive. Now you can open the door and talk to us and figure out, with us, how many of us can come in there. Or else you can just keep doing what you're doing – and we're going to *bust* our way in.

*A beat.*

MARTIN: We need some kind of a battering ram.

WEISS: We could go over to Bennett Avenue. Phil Kline has a pile of lumber in his back yard.

MARTIN: And let those people know there's a shelter on this street? We'd have a mob to contend with.

HARLOWE: We're a mob already. Listen to yourselves, listen to yourselves, all of you.

MRS. WEISS: Maybe you don't want to live, Jerry, maybe you don't care but your wife wants to live and so do your kids.

HARLOWE: Believe me, I care. I want to see the morning come too. But a mob doesn't have any brains and that's what you're proving.

HENDERSON: I agree with Jerry. Let's get hold of ourselves. Let's stop and think for a moment. Jerry, you know him better than any of us. You're his best friend. Talk to him again. Beg him. Tell him just to pick out one family, draw lots or something.

WEISS: It's got to be drawing lots. Or he'll just go ahead and pick Jerry's family.

MARTIN: It's got to be random, it's got to be fair.

MRS. WEISS: But random isn't fair. Random isn't the same thing as fair. What if it's the Hendersons. They've only been here for five years.

HENDERSON: And just what exactly does that mean.

MRS. WEISS: What do you think I think that means.

HENDERSON: I think I know what it means.

MRS. WEISS: You're a foreign person and I don't mean anything racial by that it's just a fact.

HENDERSON: I'm an American citizen. Free and clear. Same as you are.

WEISS: Yes. Absolutely. You're an American citizen. Congratulations. You probably know more about

HENDERSON: The constitution. History.

WEISS: Checks and balances what do I care.

HENDERSON: I know more about

more about your country

WEISS: Because you studied

HENDERSON: I know more about your country

WEISS: Than I do.

HENDERSON: More about your country than you do. More about your constitution, laws

WEISS: Because you *studied* it.

HARLOWE: This isn't the time for this argument.

WEISS: I don't know all of the *things* about being an American, the same way as a guy who has been *studying* them but what I know is that I have them in my *heart*, in my *soul* I am an American through and through because because because because because I don't know how to *be* any other thing. I have Democracy in my *blood.*

82

HENDERSON: Jerks like you never even *worked* to be an American barely worked *as* an American you're supposed to own the whole joint because you were born here by accident? Who is the person adding *value* to this situation? What I pay in taxes!

WEISS: You think you're better than I am because you make more money than I do? This is my *soil.* America is more, America is more than a money making machine and it's more than just a collection of statutes and norms America is a culture of freedom and ... and of values, American *values* and that's what guys like you don't get guys you just storm onto our/

HENDERSON: storm/

WEISS: storm into our country and you take and you take and what do you give? I'm sick of me saying we have a problem here and then it's I'm a racist let me tell you I don't have a problem with your race I have a problem with there are too many of you be whatever you want to be that's my feeling that's not what I care about but you're taking up more than your fair share and you're taking it away from my kids!

HARLOWE: There's room for everybody here there's room in this country for everyone

WEISS: That's what everyone says when they're shoving in, room for me room for more – well this is a nation not a clown car the entire world is not going to fit in here.

HENDERSON: And you decide American values

WEISS: Damn right I do

HENDERSON: Because you've been here –

WEISS: 1856 my great great granddaddy lands here not a penny to his name

HENDERSON: and if the men who founded this country if the religious extremists who founded this nation could see you now they'd take one look at you where is his sober suit of black that man is a Methodist these are not our people this is not our culture what has happened to our country to everything we cherish to everything we hold dear what has happened to our values we've been invaded!

MARTIN: Building this country, literally building this country, from the ground up 1856? First slave ship arrives on this soil 1619.

HENDERSON: *(To WEISS mainly.)* And you're forgetting the Indian, you're forgetting the American Indian.

MARTIN: I don't forget the American Indian I didn't have anything to do with the American Indian.

HENDERSON: What happened to the American Indian there used to be a lot of them here what happened did they all *melt?* Did they all melt away?

MRS. MARTIN: Same thing happened to the people used to live where you lived before your people got there

HENDERSON: My people have been there for thousands of years, thousands

MRS. MARTIN: Before that someone else lived there and what happened to them when your people got there they just melted away? *(To the audience.)* What about the Picts? Who here is going to own up to the *Picts,* did they just *melt?*

WEISS: You were here first so big deal you didn't decide to come here and I'm not saying slavery wasn't a terrible terrible thing it was a terrible thing we all agree about that

MRS. MARTIN: We can agree about that can we

MRS. WEISS: We most certainly *can*

WEISS: let's be realistic slavery that isn't the same as choosing to come and let's be honest about this you people don't love this country you're constantly complaining about it look I'm not saying go back to where you came from I'm just saying if you don't love a country truly love a country in your bones then it's just not your country not the same as it is for me it isn't

MRS. WEISS: And this is why I'm sick and tired of black people you can't say anything, anything you don't mean anything by it it gets construed and me I don't have a racist bone in my body I am sick and *tired,* of being construed.

MARTIN: Love it in my bones this country is *made* of my bones *I am this country* so take your chest thumping jingoism somewhere else I have earned my place here through hundreds of years of sweat and through hundreds of years of endurance and culture? Anything about this country anything and everything about this country which isn't just a half assed Europe that's *ours, all* of the music –

MRS. WEISS: Hollywood's the Jews. Hollywood's the Jews what does anyone know America from they know it from the movies Americans that's how they know America from the movies and the movies *(Triumphantly thumping her chest.)* that's us that's the *Jews!*

MARTIN: I belong here like it or not and like it or not I am the core of this nation and if anyone deserves that shelter it is *my* family.

WEISS: You're not talking about yourself you're talking about your people your history I don't care about your history

MARTIN: *Now* you don't care about history.

WEISS: *You* didn't build this country you didn't contribute to this culture you manage a TGI Fridays I don't see anyone throwing *you* to the pavement or arresting you for "driving while black" I don't care how American you are or how long your people have been here I care how long you've been on the block seven years I have a three-month-old son. I have a three-month-old son.

MARTIN: *(Shouting.)* My son is two. My girl is five.

WEISS: *(Shouting.)* You people are lazy, nothing but lazy, and you want everything for nothing!

MARTIN: *(Shouting.)* I'm the one who can support my family and you're just scraping by!

*Siren again.*

*WEISS and MARTIN drop and pound and pound and pound.*

*A moment.*

HARLOWE: Forget Kline's planks we can wrench the post off the porch that'll work.

*The men storm off, the women clutch each other.*

*From offstage – the sound of a wrenching, tearing, splitting.*

*The men return with a big porch support.*

WEISS: We got it. Me and the guys got it.

*Pounding pounding pounding on shelter door; sound of wood giving way.*

*The pounding – which we recognize from before – emanates at first from the jukebox, then from all around.*

MARTIN: Alright boys. One last heave is going to do it.

This is your last chance, Stockton. You can open up for us, or we're breaking our way in, it's your choice.

*A moment.*

*And then, as they gather their final efforts, the radio sputters to life:*

JUKEBOX: This is Conelrad. This is Conelrad. Remain tuned for an important message. Remain tuned for an important message.

The President of the United States has just announced that the objects, entering our airspace, have been definitively classed as harmless. Repeat. There are no enemy missiles approaching. Repeat. There are no enemy missiles

86

approaching. The objects are harmless, and we are in no danger. Repeat. We are in no danger. The state of emergency is now, officially, called off.

*There is a long long frozen beat and then:*

MRS. WEISS: Thank God. Oh thank God.

MARTIN: Amen to that.

MRS. WEISS: Oh thank god.

*A sort of general reaction, some embracing, some slightly wild laughter, maybe a bit of weeping.*

*This takes a bit of time.*

*Coming from that:*

*WEISS to HENDERSON, MARTIN.*

WEISS: Fellahs …

I … Look. I … I went off my rocker a little I said some things. I didn't really mean them. Not … not in any way that counts.

*Shaken, still in a state of shock, but rallying.*

HARLOWE: I don't think the boys are going to hold it against you. You don't hold it against him do you Lou? Frank?

WEISS: I said a lot of – well we were all of us, well I mean, the stress, well – I mean … well you can understand how we all blew our tops a little.

*There's a murmur of voices, a few half perfunctory nods but they're all still in a state of shock.*

HENDERSON: You're a good man Marty. You've got a big old mouth on you, but you're a good man. Deep down inside. *Way* deep down.

*WEISS laughs.*

I said a lot of things too. We all did. Heat of the moment.

*The men shake. WEISS turns to HENDERSON.*

MARTIN: *(Deadly serious.)* Don't think this is something we can drop like it didn't happen, Marty. This is something you and me are going to have to have out.

*A moment of tension.*

When we play poker next week at my place and I give your ass the thumping it truly deserves.

*General highly relieved laughter, back slapping.*

WEISS: In your *dreams*, Frank, in your wildest dreams.

*More laughter than this really warrants, more back slapping.*

*But from this:*

HARLOWE: Just I hope Bill won't hold this – well I hope he won't hold it against us.

*There's a sort of guilty pause as they all look over at the shelter door.*

*And start as the shelter door slowly opens.*

*Slowly BILL STOCKTON climbs up, and into the room.*

*His face is stone. He looks around, briefly, his eyes glancing across each face, but landing on none.*

HARLOWE: Bill, ah … Bill listen. We lost our heads alright we know that but, but I mean who wouldn't – we'll pay for the damages, Bill.

We're going to take up a collection, right away.

WEISS: Oh that's right, sure enough. We'll all put in.

*A sort of collective murmur of assent: absolutely, oh and how.*

MARTIN: You'll find you won't be out a penny, Bill, not when it's all accounted for and me and the guys will pitch in for any … for any repair work, you won't have to lift a finger.

*Another more vigorous murmur.*

HENDERSON: You've done a lot for us Bill we all know that and, you'll see, you'll see that we haven't forgotten that.

WEISS: And don't think about mowing your lawn this summer.

*A general: that's right, absolutely.*

HARLOWE: Sure me and the fellows will cover the yard work.

MRS. WEISS: I'll come over and plant ever so many tulips.

MRS. MARTIN: All the girls will.

HARLOWE: The place will be a *garden*, Bill. You can just sit back and enjoy it.

*GRACE STOCKTON follows behind BILL; he offers her his hand as she steps into the room, meeting no one's eyes. LILY is just behind, she looks only at the ground.*

WEISS: We could, we could have a block party or something tomorrow night. A big celebration. I think we rate one now.

MARTIN: *(Hearty fake laughter.)* Block party's not a bad idea!

HARLOWE: Sure! One of West Culver St.'s famous BBQs. We might even invite some of the folks over from Bennett Avenue. Show 'em how it's done.

MRS WEISS: I can make my patented pink lemonade.

MRS MARTIN: That would be wonderful! And I've been looking for an excuse to whip up another batch of my special fudge brownies.

MRS WEISS: Oh I *love* your special fudge brownies –

MRS MARTIN: They're sinful but, it's a special occasion!

MRS WEISS: Well if they're sinful I must be a proper little devil. I love them so –

*This last, intended to be especially merry, falls especially flat.*

*The family exits.*

*THE NARRATOR steps out from behind a piece of scenery, smoking.*

THE NARRATOR: Tonight's very small exercise in logic: our civilization is in peril. The enemy: not bombs or enemy armies but the power of an unseen voice, the wail of a siren, a hoarse cry of fear.

Community, amity, the altruistic impulse, all that is good and right in mankind can be obliterated by no more than an image formed in the darkest recesses of the frail human mind.

Tonight's demonstration brought to you by the concerned denizens of the –

*FlashofLightBlackout*

*Houselights up at full.*

*He is staring at the audience.*

*FlashofLightBlackout*

*House lights are out, stage is restored though dim.*

*He is gasping with surprise, reeling with shock.*

*He is orienting, muttering, but we can hear him, as if he were speaking into our ear:*

THE NARRATOR: *(Muttering.)* … I'm in the studio … I'm on the set …

*He recovers just a little, looks around him:*

… I'm in the studio … I'm on the set …

Arnie? Lamont? Buck?

Jimmy? George?

*He is circling somewhat.*

Arnie? Diane? Peggy? Buzz? Jack? Joe?

*(Rallying slightly, making a stab at it.)* Alright guys, this is some gag. Hilarious. But

enough already.

Alright, where is everybody?

*Turns around. The bar. The BARTENDER.*

*The jukebox flickers into life, glows, pulses.*

*The tune it is playing is an orchestrated version of a distinctly 21st century tune.*

BARTENDER: The Big Chief. We've been expecting you. What can I do you for?

THE NARRATOR: Paul! Christ, you threw me for a loop.

BARTENDER: I don't know any Paul, boss. But if you want to be thrown for a loop you've come to the right place.

THE NARRATOR: Don't know any Paul?

BARTENDER: Nosir.

THE NARRATOR: Oh I see. I see. That's the way you want to play it?

BARTENDER: Say, let me set you up with a nice cold one.

*A beer appears.*

THE NARRATOR: Tell me it's not a prop beer.

BARTENDER: Do I look like a man who would sell a fake beer?

THE NARRATOR: This is the one part of this I can get behind.

*He swigs it.*

BARTENDER: Oh and … your cigarette.

THE NARRATOR: My cigarette.

BARTENDER: I'm going to have to ask you to extinguish it.

THE NARRATOR: My cigarette?

BARTENDER: You can't smoke that in here of course.

THE NARRATOR: What? Says who?

BARTENDER: Laws say so. Take it outside sir, if you would.

THE NARRATOR: *(Kind of recombobulating.)* You're actually asking me to put out my cigarette.

BARTENDER: Well it is, the *law*.

THE NARRATOR: *(Fastening onto this certainty.)* Fun is fun boys and a ... gag is a gag but I'm going to have to put my foot down on this one. I don't want to throw my weight around but after all, it's my show, and if a man can't smoke on his own set –

BARTENDER: It's your set is it

THE NARRATOR: That's right.

*The phone rings.*

BARTENDER: That must be your phone then.

*The phone continues to ring. And ring.*

THE NARRATOR: *(Angrily.)* This is nuts

*He picks up the phone mid-ring.*

*We hear what he hears:*

PHONE IN THE VOICE OF THE NARRATOR: And I suppose this must be your audience.

*THE NARRATOR stiffens, turns slowly around. (As he does so the jukebox discharges some spooky theremin music.)*

*There's a blackout and a flash of light.*

*Lights up on the audience.*

*Blackout and then lights up, on the stage only.*

FORBES: Hey fellah why don't you pour another one for my good buddy Harrington, oh and Gart too, pour one for Gart too while you're at it.

*The three disappeared airmen have sauntered in.*

*GART takes a kind of swipe at FORBES.*

BARTENDER: Sure thing.

HARRINGTON: *(Offering a little snack bowl.)* Boiled peanuts?

THE NARRATOR: Ah … sure. Why not.

HARRINGTON: Pickled egg?

THE NARRATOR: I'll pass.

GART: Stale potato chips?

BARTENDER: Hey there.

THE NARRATOR: Thanks.

*GART pats a spare seat.*

GART: Plenty of room. Put up your dogs and rest for a while.

*THE NARRATOR sits beside GART.*

*MAJA has entered, and sits beside him:*

THE NARRATOR: And you I take it are not Suzanne

MAJA: Not at all.

THE NARRATOR: So tell me, Maja, what does a person do to wake up around here?

MAJA: Wake up? I suppose I should be insulted.

THE NARRATOR: Nothing personal.

MAJA: Aren't you having a nice time? If you aren't, wish it all away.

THE NARRATOR: Wish it –

MAJA: Just tell it all to stop.

*A considering beat.*

THE NARRATOR: Stop.

*Everything freezes.*

*(Impressed.)* Huh.

MAJA: Now wave your right hand.

*He does so, it all resumes.*

THE NARRATOR: *(Interested.)* Huh.

MAJA: Wonderful! Now: make me disappear. Just wave your left hand.

THE NARRATOR: *(More pleasant statement than flirtation.)* If I'm going to dream, I may as well dream.

MAJA: Oh you can bring me back again. Any time.

THE NARRATOR: Wave my left hand. Up and down? Back and forth? All around?

MAJA: Something … impressive.

THE NARRATOR: All right …

*He comes up with an impressive gesture:*

Disappear.

*She doesn't.*

MAJA: Maybe later.

THE NARRATOR: Say … whose dream is it anyway?

MAJA: Shhhhhh. The act's beginning.

BARTENDER: Little girl. Shot of whiskey for your friend there?

*The LITTLE GIRL has been setting up. Seating herself carefully on a chair. Unlocking the case and placing Napoleon carefully on her lap.*

*The DUMMY is inert. Head slack.*

*The rest of the inhabitants of the bar have filtered in: THE BIG HEADED ALIEN, the BANDAGED LADY ,etc.*

LITTLE GIRL: Not until after the act, thank you.

BARTENDER: Suit yourself. The floor is yours sweetheart.

*Lights rise blindingly on the LITTLE GIRL and the DUMMY.*

*She smiles confidently at the audience.*

*Looks at Napoleon expectantly.*

*Looks at audience. Looks at Napoleon.*

*She coughs loudly. Then:*

LITTLE GIRL: ahem

*Nothing.*

Napoleon. Napoooooleon. Hallo.

*She knocks on the side of his head.*

Anybody home? Anybody home in there?

Wake up. Wakey wakey wakey.

*Napoleon's eye's flick open.*

There you are.

Say Napoleon, these people all came to see you!

Isn't that just great? Better treat them nicely.

DUMMY: Where's my whiskey.

LITTLE GIRL: *(Sotto voce.)* We said after the act.

DUMMY: Whiskey! Whiskey! Whiskey!

LITTLE GIRL: We came to entertain the nice people Napoleon, remember?

DUMMY: Whiskey! Whiskey! Whiskey!

*A beat.*

LITTLE GIRL: A shot of whiskey please. Straight up.

BARTENDER: *(To THE NARRATOR.)* Say, it's a great gag isn't it?

Shot of whiskey coming right up!

DUMMY: And make it a double.

BARTENDER: Sure thing! *(To THE NARRATOR.)* "Make it a double."

Kid slays me! Kid slays me!

Here you go little lady. A double,
on the double.

DUMMY: Leave the wisecracks, to the professional.

*BARTENDER chortles.*

*She pours the whiskey down his gullet.*

That's more like it! Entertainment: coming right up!

ahem ahem ahem

*He launches into a very rusty set of scales:*

mi mi mi mi mi mi mi mi mi mi … .

LITTLE GIRL: *(Alarmed.)* Napoleon you aren't going to *sing are you?*

DUMMY: A deal is, as they say, a deal.

LITTLE GIRL: *(Gesturing towards the audience.)* Napoleon, look at how nice the people are!

They don't want to hear you sing.

DUMMY: Course they do, Sweetheart, course they do.
Except that guy. Hey bud – bud – you a regular here?

THE NARRATOR: Me?

BARTENDER: He's here every night.

*THE NARRATOR whips around to stare at him.*

THE NARRATOR: I am?

DUMMY: Say what's your gambit, mister?

THE NARRATOR: What's my …

DUMMY: Your game, your rigamarole, your hustle?

Watchu do.

THE NARRATOR: Oh. Well I make TV.

DUMMY: The little big pictures, eh?

THE NARRATOR: Something like that.

DUMMY: I know them well. Accounts for my size.

*(Doing Gloria Swanson: )*

*"I'm big! It's just the picture that is small!"*

*Ha ha ha ha ha ha ha –*

*Everyone joins in the laughter, genially.*

And what do you do for the TV. Janitor? Night clerk?

THE NARRATOR: I'm a writer.

DUMMY: Worse and worse. Kinda sharp looking, for a writer.

THE NARRATOR: Well, I also appear on camera at the
    beginning and the end of the show.

DUMMY: Is that right.

THE NARRATOR: Well it's my own show, you see.

DUMMY: Your own show eh. Me, I would have said

    that was a presumption but what do I know.

Me I'm just a brash stick of kindling

a splinter with a few big ideas

But that explains the stink-eye when it comes

to the singing, sure, you're more of a story man.

Hey there then how's about *this for a story:*

*He snaps his fingers.*

*SANDY enters the stage, looking just as we last saw her, only she is wearing a glamorous silver sheath.*

SANDY: General … Walters?

GENERAL WALTERS: Miss Horn.

DUMMY: You recognize the girl?

THE NARRATOR: Never seen her before in my life.

DUMMY: Well take a good long look because later on you're going to tell everyone you wrote her.

*GENERAL WALTERS smiles.*

GENERAL WALTERS: You look very well. You look just fine.

Which must sound idiotic but, what do you say to someone who's just had a fifty-two year sleep? Let's just say: we were very relieved to find you still alive. Cryo technology was really just in its infancy when you, well when you began your … I suppose I must call it a kind of journey.

SANDY: I feel – rested.

GENERAL WALTERS: Yes. Of course. And you've been well looked after? I hope you *(She waves her hands about loosely indicating SANDY's outfit.)* my secretary seemed to think that your original articles of clothing, although well stored and intact, would no longer be, as she put it, of "any real use whatsoever".

SANDY: This is just fine.

GENERAL WALTERS: Wonderful.

*She has unfortunately run out of things to say and before she can regroup SANDY jumps into the breach.*

SANDY: General, I was told that Commander Stansfield –

GENERAL WALTERS: His ship landed twelve hours ago.

SANDY: I'm very eager to see him.

GENERAL WALTERS: Of course you are. Miss Horn, I asked to see you.

SANDY: Is he alright?

GENERAL WALTERS: Commander Stansfield is in good health. Naturally, he's very tired. A trifle disoriented.

SANDY: I must see him.

GENERAL WALTERS: I had to talk to you.

SANDY: *(This is only slightly a question.)* He did … complete his mission.

GENERAL WALTERS: He did reach the other galaxy, the other solar system. He landed. And he took off again. There was no life. We found that out ourselves, of course, thirty years ago, from the comfort of our desks here at home. One of the ironies of our progress.

Another irony of our progress, or. I suppose it isn't really, strictly speaking an irony. I suppose it is, straight out, a ferocious travesty of fate. Commander Stansfield's Cryo unit began its initial sequencing, and everything was proceeding smoothly, but before the immersion completed, the process was aborted. Manually. By Commander Stansfield himself.

SANDY: So you mean to tell me

GENERAL WALTERS: Yes, Miss Horn. I'm afraid I do.

*A beat.*

SANDY: I know why he did it.

*Her head goes down, her eyes close.*

God help me, I know why.

GENERAL WALTERS: Upon landing, his first question was to ask after you. I told him what had occurred.

SANDY: I want – I very much want to see him.

GENERAL WALTERS: Commander Stansfield has asked, that you respect his wish to not see you again.

SANDY: Oh, no. No. What happened. It doesn't make a difference.

GENERAL WALTERS: I'm afraid it does. Fifty years, Miss Horn. In the cockpit of a ship. Fifty years.

His loneliness must have been something brand-new in human experience.

SANDY: General Walters. I'll go away again if he wants me to. I must see him again. Only one time.

GENERAL WALTERS: I'm afraid it's impossible. I wish that it was not.

*SANDY presses her hands to her face.*

You're still young, and beautiful Miss Horn. There's a whole new world out there for you to explore. I hope you can think of it, well as a kind of adventure. A discovery.

*She looks up.*

SANDY: A whole new world … in which I don't know a single soul. An adventure … I suppose it will be a kind of adventure. One I'll embark upon, entirely alone.

I suppose I will try to think of it, as a kind of mystery. One I'll hope to have the patience for. All the patience in the universe.

GENERAL WALTERS: What's that, Miss Horn?

SANDY: Goodbye, General Walters.

*She departs.*

*After a moment:*

GENERAL WALTERS: You may come out now, Commander Stansfield, she's gone.

*An OLD MAN steps from backstage.*

GENERAL WALTERS: Perhaps you'll relent Commander, and meet with her. Only once. Let her hear it from your own lips.

*STANSFIELD shakes his head.*

*After a moment:*

GENERAL WALTERS: And now that you've seen her commander, tell me. Was she the woman you stayed awake to dream of, all those fifty-two lonely years?

*A long beat.*

*The OLD MAN nods.*

*The DUMMY lifts up his arms, as a conductor does; when he lowers them the inhabitants of the bar begin to sing*

Don't be afraid to dream
But remember when you do
That everything you dream
Is also dreaming you …

*The song concludes.*

*THE NARRATOR steps forward.*

THE NARRATOR: Commander Douglas Stansfield. Sandra Horn. A couple of forgotten pioneers of the Space Age. We have just witnessed a few select moments of their existence, a kind of haiku of character and circumstance. Exceptional individuals whose achievements will never make the grade for any book of history, but which are already marked down in the ledgers of a very different kind of institution, one located in –

Ladies and Gentlemen, it is our fond and fervent hope that this evening has been an entertainment. But I am tasked in tonight's conclusionary remarks with a little hectoring reminder, a note that the imagination seldom yields to reason, rather, it is reason, perpetually, which yields to the imagination.

The moments when we feel ourselves most awake we are often as good as dreaming; and our most outlandish speculations –

*And here he makes a gesture which includes the audience.*

– are often true. In a few moments the show will end and after a round of very vigorous applause you will gather your belongings and make your way to the lobby –

*From the lobby we hear the sound of an astonishing and unearthly machine; blue light and possibly also smoke seeps from the edges of the door ...*

*He makes a short and elaborate but decisive gesture. The machine, the light, the smoke cease instantly.*

*He takes just a microsecond to recalibrate.*

you'll make your way into the lobby

*From the lobby: the Void Werewolf, even more fearsome, howling and snuffling right at the door, pawing at it, a red light seeps from the edges ...*

*He waves his hands about in a way which is admittedly slightly wide and wheeling*

*Instantly, the lobby quiets.*

you will exit into the lobby.

*He halts for just a microsecond, continues.*

You remember the lobby. Stylish. Clean. Perfectly safe.
Nice men and women offering you food and drink for sale
– have a glass of pinot, and an ice cream –

*And now the sound of a strange and wonderful meadow, just
beautiful, astonishing birds, white light, possibly a meadow in space,
and from it arising the sounds of a vast crowd a party a thronging ...*

*he tries a very definite looking kind of sideways swipe.*

*Nothing.*

*He tries another gesture. Nothing. Another.*

*The lobby only grows in volume, and perhaps begins to seep, softly,
from other areas of the theater itself. As he looks around in alarm
MAJA laughs, snaps her fingers, and the sound entirely ceases.*

And as you exit the building be assured that you will not
plummet into an endless field of stars; you'll step onto
pavement and wend your way home, tuck yourself into
your warm bed which will be exactly where you left it and
on the same planet, your partner is entirely what he or she
seems, and when you wake up in the morning you will
have the same identity you had when you went to sleep.

Nonetheless Ladies and Gentlemen, though it is a hoary
commonplace of the theater it is in fact true that with no
more than a few frail bodies, the shifting of artificial light
and electronic sound, fabric, plywood, can-do and, most
importantly, your own mental technology, we have created
aliens, a living dream, an imaginary child, a dimensional
vortex, men winking out of existence, Armageddon,
America, an unprecedented feat of human endurance and
love and, I suppose, if the truth were to be told, yours truly.

It is time to acknowledge that we are a dreaming species in
an imaginary country and fantasy is the coin of the realm;
we have an unquenchable appetite for the extraordinary
and our connection to reality is tenuous at best.

Call it our greatest weakness, call it our greatest strength, we are all of us traveling in a place where the impossible, is the actual. In a middle ground between light and shadow, science and superstition. A region as vast as space and as timeless as infinity a place where the pit of man's fears collide with the height of his aspiration, an area of the incredible. We are all of us, each and every one of us, card carrying citizens of

the Twilight Zone.

END